WHAT HAPPENED NEXT WAS ABSOLUTELY IMPOSSIBLE . . .

The Tralthan physician swayed alarmingly on its six stubby legs, then toppled with a crash. A few yards away, the Melfan doctor subsided slowly as its multi-jointed legs turned limp; the Kelgian theater nurse slipped to the floor, its silvery fur undulating as if affected by a tiny whirlwind; and a human member of the transfer team standing next to Conway dropped loosely to his hands and knees, then rolled onto his side.

The unknown patient on the table had brought something into the operating room that was menacing the lives of members of four totally different species—and no known organism in the universe could do that!

"Sound the alarm for Contamination One!" Conway yelled into his speaker—knowing sickly that he was condemning to death half the medical staff in the room . . .

Also by James White
Published by Ballantine Books:

AMBULANCE SHIP

JAMES WHITE

A Del Rey Book

BALLANTINE BOOKS • NEW YORK

To Jack Cohen
Who is a stickler for xenobiological verisimilitude,
In appreciation

CONTENTS

The Secret History
of Sector General

For a series that began twenty years ago and has so far run to over a quarter of a million words, Sector General got off to a very shaky start. In fact, had the late and sadly missed Ted Carnell, who was at that time the editor of the British sf magazine, *New Worlds,* not been desperate to fill a 17,000-word hole which had opened up in his November 1957 issue, the first novelette in the series, "Sector General," would not have been accepted without literary surgery of a drastic nature.

The birth of the Sector General idea was a natural, if perhaps a premature, occurrence. I had been writing professionally for just over four years and the joins were still showing in my work. But even in those early apprenticeship days I had a strong preference for medics or extraterrestrials as the chief characters in my stories, and gradually both types began appearing in the same stories. For example, in the Ballantine collection *The Aliens Among Us* there was a story called "To Kill or Cure," which dealt with the fumbling attempts of a navy doctor from a rescue helicopter to give medical assistance to the survivor of a crashed extraterrestrial spaceship. So it was only natural that a story that dealt with the problems inherent in human beings treating large numbers of extraterrestrial patients in hospital conditions, and aliens treating humans, would evolve.

The novelette "Sector General," however, had flaws. Ted Carnell said that it lacked a coherent plot; that the principal character, Doctor Conway, simply drifted into and out of medical situations without solving his main problem—the ethical conflict in his mind between the militaristic Monitor Corps, which maintained the hospital, and its intensely pacifist medical staff; and that the whole thing was so episodic that it resembled an interstellar *Emergency Ward 10,* a very corny British TV hospital series of the time. Comparing that series to my story was surely the unkindest surgical incision of all! He also said that I had spelled *efficient* two different ways in the story, and both ways were wrong. There were other flaws that became apparent only with hindsight, but these were corrected in the later stories of the series.

But Ted did like the basic idea. He said that the background of the huge hospital in space was one that I should keep going, if only occasionally. He also said that Harry Harrison had called him at his office and was somewhat irritated with me for beating him to the punch with the interstellar hospital idea, because he had been planning a series of four or five short stories with just such a background, reckoning that it was a new idea. Harry still intended doing the stories, Ted said, but his enthusiasm had been blunted.

This last piece of news scared me half to death.

At that time I had not met Harry Harrison, but I knew quite a lot about him. I knew since reading *Rockdiver* as a very young fan that he had been one of my favorite authors; that he spoke rather loudly to people when he was roused; and that he was probably *Deathworld* on two feet. And there was I, a fan and a professional writer still wet behind the ears, having the effrontery to actually blunt *his* enthusiasm! But Harry must be a truly kind and forgiving soul because nothing catastrophic has happened to me. At least not yet.

All the same, there must be a probability world somewhere in which he got in first with the idea and blunted my enthusiasm, and the sf shelves in the bookshops carry a series of books by Harry Harrison about an interstellar hospital. If someone would invent a transverse time-travel machine, I should dearly like to borrow it for a few hours to buy those books.

The second story in the series was "Trouble With Emily" and Ted was much happier with this one. It featured Doctor Conway—carrying a pint-sized alien with psi powers on his shoulder instead of a large chip —and a party of Monitor Corpsmen, who were assisting him with the treatment of a brontosaurus-like patient called Emily, because one of the Corps officers had a fondness for reading the Bronte sisters.

But the function of the Monitor Corps, the law enforcement and executive arm of the Galactic Federation whose sixty-odd intelligent species were represented on the staff of Sector General, was something that needed clarification, I thought. The result was a very long novelette of some 21,000 words.

Essentially the Monitor Corps was a police force on an interstellar scale, but I did not want them to be the usual ruthless, routine-indoctrinated, basically stupid organization that is so handy to have around when an idealistic principal character needs a bit of ethical conflict. Conway was one of the good guys and I wanted them to be good guys too, but with different ideas as to the kind of activity that produces the greater good.

Their duties included interstellar survey and first-contact work as well as maintaining the Federation's peace—a job that could, if they were unable to discourage the warmongers, give rise to a police action that was indistinguishable from an act of war. But the Corps much preferred to wage psychological warfare aimed at discouraging planetary and interplanetary violence and when, despite their efforts, a war broke out, then they very closely monitored the beings who were waging it.

These warlike entities belonged to a psychological rather than physiological classification, and regardless of species they were the classification responsible for most of the trouble within the Federation. The story told of the efforts of the Monitor Corps first to attempt to prevent the war and then damp down the war, and

Conway and Sector General came into it only when things went catastrophically wrong and large numbers of human and e-t casualties had to be dealt with. The original title of the story was "Classification: Warrior."

Ted, however, insisted that it was much too serious a story to be tied into the *Sector General* series, and he had me delete all references to the Monitor Corps (rechristening them the Stellar Guard), the Federation, Sector General hospital and Conway. The story was retitled "Occupation: Warrior." It appeared in the collection *The Aliens Among Us,* which also contained a proper Sector General story called "Countercharm."

With the next story, "Visitor at Large," later published in the collection entitled *Hospital Station,* the series was firmly back on the rails. Appearing for the first time in the hospital was the insectile, incredibly fragile and emotion-sensitive Doctor Prilicla, who was later to become the most popular character in the series. The patient that Conway and Prilicla were treating was physically incapable of becoming sick, although it was, of course, subject to psychological disturbances. This particular patient was amoebic, highly adaptable and had the ability to extrude any limbs or sensory organs required for any given situation. It reproduced by fission and inherited at the time of its "birth" all of the experience and knowledge of its parent, and of its parent's parent, and on back to the beginning of its evolution. The creature's problem was that it had suffered a trauma that had caused it to withdraw from all outside contact and it was slowly dissolving into water; and water turned out to be the solution in both senses of the word.

The next story featured a jump backwards in time to the period when the hospital was under construction, and the central character was O'Mara, who was later to become its Chief Psychologist. This was followed by a story that featured a patient with a most distressing collection of symptoms, which Conway steadfastly, and against all the advice and direct orders of his superiors, refused to treat. The stories were called "Medic" and "Outpatient" respectively, and they also appeared in the *Hospital Station* collection, which contained all five of the Sector General stories written at that time.

Around this time the one-hundredth issue of *New Worlds* was coming up and Ted Carnell had been writing to his regular authors asking them to produce something special for it. I submitted a 14,000-worder called "The Apprentice"—it later appeared in my *Monsters and Medics* collection—which he straightaway stuck into issue 99 because, he said, he had only a 7,000-word hole left in number 100. Could I fill it with a Sector General short story, within three weeks?

I badly wanted to make it into that one-hundredth issue with its lineup of top authors, but I did not have a single alien ailment in my head. In desperation I tried to build a story around an Earth-human condition that might have an extraterrestrial equivalent, an ailment of which I had firsthand experience, diabetes.

Now there is no great problem in pushing a hypodermic needle through the tegument and subcutaneous tissue of an Earth-human and injecting a measured dose of insulin—except sometimes I go "Ouch." But suppose the diabetic patient was a crab-like life-form, whose limbs and body were covered by a hard shell? Obviously the same procedure would not be suitable, unless one used a sterile power drill and even this, in time, would lead to grave weakening of the body structure by leaving it in the condition of an exoskeletal sieve. Solving this problem, with the help of a magnificently proportioned nurse and later an e-t pathologist called Murchison, was the plot line for the story "Countercharm," which dropped nicely into Ted's 7,000-word hole as well as appearing later in *The Aliens Among Us* collection.

Probably the next idea for the series came about because of a second or third re-reading of Hal Clement's *Needle*. The situation was that a Very Important Extraterrestrial Person had had a disagreement with its personal medic and as a result had been admitted to the hospital. Only much later in the story did Conway discover that the medic in question was an intelligent, organized virus life-form who lived and worked inside its patient. The story was called, inevitably, "Resident Physician" and was an introductory novelette to the first, and so far the only, Sector General novel-length work, "Field Hospital." "Resident Physician" and "Field Hospital" were later published together as *Star Surgeon*.

Normally I do not like stories of violence or the senseless killing that is war. But if a story is to hold the interest of the reader there must be conflict, which means violence or struggle of some kind. However, in a medical sf story of the Sector General type the violence is usually the direct or indirect result of a natural catastrophe, a disaster in space or an epidemic of some kind. And if there *is* a war situation of the kind that occurred in *Star Surgeon*, then the medics are fighting only to save lives, and the Monitor Corps, like the good little policemen they are, are fighting to stop the war rather than win it—which is the essential difference between maintaining the peace and waging a war.

There is not enough space to go into the plot details of *Star Surgeon*, but one should be mentioned. In "Occupation: Warrior," which should have been the fourth Sector General story, "Classification: Warrior," the leading character was a tactician called Dermod; and the same character turned up again as the Monitor Corps Fleet Commander who defended the hospital in *Star Surgeon* as well as having an important part to play in *Major Operation.* I don't know why I went to the trouble of establishing this tenuous connection between the series proper and the Sector General story that had been deliberately de-Sector Generalized, but it seemed important to me at the time.

There was a four-year gap before the next stories in the series were written. These were five novelettes that were planned, like the *Ambulance Ship* trio, to build progressively into a novel. They were "Invader," "Vertigo," "Blood Brother," "Meatball" and "Major Operation," and with linking material added they were published as the book-length *Major Operation.*

"Invader" set the stage by introducing to the hospital a thought-controlled tool that caused havoc until Conway realized how valuable such a device could be in the hands of a surgeon who fully understood its uses. During further investigation of the planet on which the tool originated, the Monitor Corps rescued a doughnut-shaped alien who had to roll all the time to live because it did not have a heart but depended on a gravity feed system for blood circulation. This story was called "Vertigo," and the alien was a present of my friend Bob Shaw, who called it a Drambon.

Bob thought it might be fun if I used his e-t and called it a Drambon because he had used the Drambon species in one of his stories; then we could wait and see how long it would take one of the science-fiction buffs to spot the fact that a certain extraterrestrial had cropped up, or rather rolled up, in the work of two different authors. But up until now the widely traveled Drambon life-form seems to have gone unspotted.

The next story in the series derived from an original idea by a well-known English fan of the time, Ken Cheslin. We were at a convention party when he said, as nearly as I can remember, "James, you know how doctors used to be called leeches? Why don't you write a story where the doctor really *is* a leech?" The e-t that resulted was a life-form whose method of treatment was to withdraw practically all of its patient's blood—a very disconcerting process for the being concerned—and remove the offending toxic material or micro-organisms before returning the blood to the patient good as new. The story was called "Blood Brother." Thanks, Ken.

Regarding "Meatball" and the climactic "Major Operation," there is very little to say except that the poisoned and polluted living planet that was the patient in those stories required treatment on such a vast scale that the operation was a military as well as a medical one.

The next story in the series, so far published only in Britain in *New Writings in SF 22,* was called "Spacebird." The idea for an organic, completely non-metallic spaceship had been in my notebook for a long time, but it could not be used until I could discover a means of boosting such a bird to escape velocity. Then at one of the conventions I mentioned my problem to Jack Cohen. Jack, who is a very helpful person and a stickler for xenobiological verisimilitude, is senior lecturer in animal reproduction at the University of Birmingham in England. He knows so much about strange and alien life-forms that, when asked if a certain hypothetical extraterrestrial is physiologically possible, he invariably cites examples of a couple of terrestrial life-forms that are even weirder. The answer to my problem, Jack said, was the bombardier beetle —a small, mid-European insect that, when threatened with danger, expels and ignites gas from its rear so violently that it lands many inches away.

When the story was written, the launching of the spacecraft was from a Mesklin-type planet with high centrifugal force and low gravity at its equator to aid the process; and it was with millions of outsize bombardier beetles forming the multistaging sequences, all blasting away and hoisting the bird into space. Surely this was an idea to arouse the sense of wonder, I thought. Think of the technological achievement it represented for a race completely without metals, and think of the timing and delicacy of control involved. Try not to think of the smell . . .

The latest stories to be written are the three linked which comprise the book you are about to read. It deals with a new aspect of the work at Sector General —the hospital's special ambulance service—and concerns the extraterrestrial medical, physiological, psychological and engineering problems that must be solved, quickly and on the site of the accident by the ambulance ship's crew if the casualties are to survive until they reach the hospital. When these problems arise, the ambulance ships are inevitably far removed from the virtually limitless facilities of Sector General, so the alien technologists and medical specialists of the crews concerned must fall back on their own ingenuity and strictly limited resources. If they make a wrong decision, the consequences can be far-reaching indeed.

To date the Sector General series has run to one short story, fifteen novelettes and one novel. I hope to go on writing about extraterrestrials, their exotic physiologies, their alien viewpoints and the problems of communication and understanding they represent. But my problem in recent years has been that, when I dream up a really alien alien, it promptly falls sick or gets itself damaged in an accident and ends up becoming a problem for Sector Twelve General Hospital.

AMBULANCE
SHIP

PART ONE

Contagion

Senior Physician Conway wriggled into a slightly less uncomfortable position in a piece of furniture that had been designed for the comfort of a six-legged, exoskeletal Melfan, and said in an aggrieved tone, "After twelve years' medical and surgical experience in the Federation's biggest multienvironment hospital, one would expect the next logical step up the promotional ladder would be to something more prestigious than . . . than an ambulance driver!"

There was no immediate response from the other four beings who were waiting with him in the office of the Chief Psychologist. Doctor Prilicla clung silently to the ceiling, the position it favored when in the company of more massive and well-muscled beings than itself. Sharing an Illensan bench were the spectacularly beautiful Pathologist Murchison and a silver-furred, caterpiller-like Kelgian charge nurse called Naydrad, also in silence. It was Major Fletcher, who as a recent visitor to the hospital had been given the office's only physiologically suitable chair, who broke the silence.

Seriously, he said, "You will not be allowed to drive, Doctor."

It was plain that Major Fletcher was still very conscious of the bright new ship commander's insignia decorating the sleeve of his Monitor Corps tunic, and that he was already concerned about the welfare of the vessel so soon to be his. Conway remembered feeling the same way about his first pocket scanner.

"Not even an ambulance driver," said Murchison, laughing.

Naydrad joined the conversation with a series of moaning, whistling sounds, which translated as, "In an establishment like this one, Doctor, do you expect logic?"

Conway did not reply. He was thinking that the hospital grapevine, a normally dependable form of vegetable life, had been carrying the news for days that a senior physician, Conway himself, was to be permanently attached to an ambulance ship.

On the ceiling, Doctor Prilicla was beginning to quiver in response to his emotional radiation, so Conway tried to bring his feelings of confusion and disappointment and hurt pride under control.

"Please do not concern yourself unnecessarily over this matter, friend Conway," said the little empath, the musical trills and clicks of its Cinrusskin speech overlaying the emotionless translated words. "We have yet to be informed officially of the new assignment, and the probability is that you may be pleasantly surprised, Doctor."

Prilicla, Conway knew, was not averse to telling lies if by so doing it could improve the emotional atmosphere of a situation. But not if the improvement would last for only a few seconds or minutes and be followed by even more intense feelings of anger and disappointment.

"What makes you think so, Doctor?" Conway asked. "You used the word *probability* and not *possibility*. Have you inside information?"

"That is correct, friend Conway," the Cinrusskin replied. "I have detected a source of emotional radiation that entered the outer office several minutes ago. It is identifiable as belonging to the Chief Psychologist, and the emoting is purposeful, with the type of minor-key worrying associated with the carriage of authority and responsibility. I cannot detect the kind of feelings that should be present if the imparting of unpleasant news to someone was being planned. At present Major O'Mara is talking to an assistant, who is also unaware of any potential unpleasantness."

Conway smiled and said, "Thank you, Doctor. I feel much better now."

"I know," said Prilicla.

"And I feel," said Nurse Naydrad, "that such discussion of the being O'Mara's feelings verges on a breach of medical ethics. Emotional radiation is privileged information, surely, and should not be divulged in this fashion."

"Perhaps you have not considered the fact," Prilicla replied, using the form of words which was the closest it could ever come to telling another being it was wrong, "that the being whose emotional radiation was under discussion is not a patient, friend Naydrad, and that the being most closely resembling a patient in this situation is Doctor Conway, who is concerned about the future and requires reassurance in the form of information on the non-patient's emotional radiation . . . "

Naydrad's silvery fur was beginning to twitch and ripple, indicating that the Kelgian charge nurse was about to reply. But the entrance of the non-patient from the outer office put an end to what could have been an interesting ethical debate.

O'Mara nodded briefly to everyone in turn, and took the only other physiologically suitable seat in the room, his own. The Chief Psychologist's features were about as readable as a lump of weathered basalt, which in some respects they resembled, but the eyes which regarded them were backed by a mind so keenly analytical that it gave O'Mara what amounted to a telepathic faculty.

Caustically, he began: "Before I tell you why I have asked for you four in particular to accompany Major Fletcher, and give you the details of your next assignment, which no doubt you have already learned in outline, I have to give you some background information of a non-medical nature.

"The problem of briefing people like yourselves on this subject," he went on, "is that I cannot afford to make assumptions regarding your level of ignorance in matters outside your specialties. Should some of this information seem too elementary, you are at liberty to allow your attention to wander, so long as I don't catch you at it."

"You have our undivided attention, friend O'Mara," said Prilicla, who, of course, knew this to be a fact.

"For the time being," Naydrad added.

"Charge Nurse Naydrad!" Major Fletcher burst out, his reddening face clashing with the dark green of his uniform. "You are being something less than respectful to a senior officer. Such offensive behavior will not be tolerated on my ship, nor shall I—"

O'Mara held up his hand and said dryly, "I didn't take offense, Major, and neither should you. Up until now, your career has been free of close personal contact with e-ts, so your mistake is understandable. It is unlikely to be repeated when you learn to understand the thought processes and behavior of the beings who will be working with you on this project.

"Charge Nurse Naydrad," O'Mara went on, politely for him, "is a Kelgian, a caterpillar-like lifeform whose most noticeable feature is an all-over coat of silver-gray fur. You will already have noticed that Naydrad's fur is constantly in motion, as if a strong wind was continually blowing it into tufts and ripples. These are completely involuntary movements triggered by its emotional reactions to outside stimuli. The evolutionary reasons for this mechanism are not clearly understood, not even by the Kelgians themselves, but it is generally believed that the emotionally expressive fur complements the Kelgian vocal equipment, which lacks emotional flexibility of tone. However, you must understand that the movements of the fur makes it absolutely clear to another Kelgian what it feels about the subject under discussion. As a result, they always say exactly what they mean because what they think is plainly obvious—at least to another Kelgian. They cannot do otherwise. Unlike Doctor Prilicla, who is always polite and sometimes edits the truth to remove the unpleasant bits, Charge Nurse Naydrad will invariably tell the truth regardless of your rank or your feelings. You will soon grow used to it, Major.

"But I did not intend to give a lecture on Kelgians," he continued. "I did intend to discuss briefly the formation of what is now called the Galactic Federation . . . "

On the briefing screen behind him there appeared suddenly a three-dimensional representation of the galactic double spiral with its major stellar features and the edge of a neighboring galaxy, shown at distances that were not to scale. As they watched and listened a short, bright line of yellow light appeared near the rim, then another and another—the links between Earth and the early Earth-seeded colonies, and the systems of Orligia and Nidia, which were the first extraterrestrial cultures to be contacted. Another cluster of yellow lines appeared, the worlds colonized or contacted by Traltha.

Several decades had passed before the worlds available to the Orligians, Nidians, Tralthans and Earth-humans were made available to each other. (Beings tended to be suspicious in those days, on one occasion even to the point of war.) But time as well as distance was being compressed on this representation.

The tracery of golden lines grew more rapidly as contact, then commerce, was established with the highly advanced and stable cultures of Kelgia, Illensa, Hudlar, Melf and, if any, their associated colonies. Visually it did not seem to be an orderly progression. The lines darted inwards to the galactic center, doubled back to the rim, seesawed between zenith and nadir, and even made a jump across intergalactic space to link up with the Ian worlds—although in that instance it had been the Ians who had done the initial traveling. When the lines connected the worlds of the Galactic Federation, the planets known to contain intelligent and, in their own sometimes peculiar fashions, technically and philosophically advanced life, the result was an untidy yellow scribble resembling a cross between a DNA molecule and a bramble bush.

" . . . Only a tiny fraction of the Galaxy has been explored by us or by any of the other races within the

Federation," O'Mara continued, "and we are in the position of a man who has friends in far countries but has no idea of who is living in the next street. The reason for this is that travelers tend to meet more often than people who stay at home, especially when the travelers exchange addresses and visits regularly . . . "

Providing there were no major distorting influences en route and the exact co-ordinates of the destination were known, it was virtually as easy to travel through subspace to a neighboring solar system as to one at the other end of the Galaxy. But one had first to find an inhabited solar system before its co-ordinates could be logged, and that was proving to be no easy task.

Very, very slowly, a few of the smaller blank areas in the star charts were being mapped and surveyed, but with little success. When the survey scoutships turned up a star with planets, it was a rare find—even rarer when the planets included one harboring life. And if one of the native life-forms was intelligent, jubilation, not unmixed with concern over what might be a possible threat to the Pax Galactica, swept the worlds of the Federation. Then the Cultural Contact specialists of the Monitor Corps were sent to perform the tricky, time-consuming and often dangerous job of establishing contact in depth.

The Cultural Contact people were the elite of the Monitor Corps, a small group of specialists in e-t communications, philosophy and psychology. Although small, the group was not, regrettably, overworked . . .

" . . . During the past twenty years," O'Mara went on, "they have initiated First Contact procedure on three occasions, all of which resulted in the species concerned joining the Federation. I will not bore you with details of the number of survey operations mounted and the ships, personnel and materiel involved, or shock you with the cost of it all. I mention the Cultural Contact group's three successes simply to make the point that within the same time period this hospital became fully operational and also initiated First Contacts, which resulted in seven new species joining the Federation. This was accomplished not by a slow, patient buildup and widening of communications until the exchange of complex philosophical and sociological concepts became possible, but by giving medical assistance to a sick alien."

The Chief Psychologist stared at each of them in turn, and it was obvious that he did not need Prilicla to tell him that he had their undivided attention. "I'm oversimplifying, of course. You had the medical and/or surgical problem of treating a hitherto unknown life-form. You had the hospital's translation computer, the second largest in the Galaxy, and Monitor Corps communications specialists to assist where necessary. Indeed, the Corps was responsible for rescuing many of the extraterrestrial casualties. But the fact remains that all of us, by giving medical assistance, demonstrated the Federation's good will towards e-ts much more simply and directly than could have been done by any long-winded exchange of concepts. As a result, there has recently been a marked change of emphasis in First Contact policy . . . "

Just as there was only one known way of traveling in hyperspace, there was only one method of sending a distress signal if an accident or malfunction occurred and a vessel was stranded in normal space between the stars. Tight-beam subspace radio was not a dependable method of interstellar communication, subject as it was to interference and distortion caused by intervening stellar bodies, as well as requiring inordinate amounts of a vessel's power—power which a distressed ship was unlikely to have available. But a distress beacon did not have to carry intelligence. It was simply a nuclear-powered device which broadcast a location signal, a subspace scream for help, which ran up and down the usable frequencies until, in a matter of minutes or hours, it died.

Because all Federation ships were required to file course and passenger details before departure, the position of the distress signal was usually a good indication of the physiological type of species that had run into trouble, and an ambulance ship with a matching crew and life-support equipment was sent from Sector General or from the ship's home planet.

But there were instances, far more than were generally realized, when the disasters involved beings unknown to the Federation in urgent need of help, help which the would-be rescuers were powerless to give.

Only when the rescue ship concerned had the capability of extending its hyperdrive envelope to include the distressed vessel, or when the beings could be extricated safely and a suitable environment prepared for them within the Federation ship, were they transported to Sector General. The result was that many hitherto unknown life-forms, being of high intelligence and advanced technology, were lost except as interesting specimens for dissection and study. But an answer to this problem had been sought and, perhaps, found.

It had been decided to equip one very special ambulance ship that would answer only those distress signals whose positions did not agree with the flight plans filed by Federation vessels.

" . . . Whenever possible," O'Mara continued, "we prefer to make contact with a star-traveling race. Species who are intelligent but are not space travelers pose problems. We are never sure whether we are helping or hindering their natural development, giving them a technological leg up or a crushing inferiority complex when we drop down from their sky—"

Naydrad broke in: "The starship in distress might not possess a beacon. What then?"

"If a species advanced enough to possess starships did not make this provision for the safety of its individuals," O'Mara replied, "then I would prefer not to know them."

"I understand," said the Kelgian.

The Chief Psychologist nodded, then went on briskly, "Now you know why four senior or specialist members of the hospital's medical and surgical services are being demoted to ambulance attendants." He tapped buttons on his desk, and the Federation star map was replaced by a large and detailed diagram of a ship. "Attendants on a very special ambulance, as you can see. Captain Fletcher, continue, please."

For the first time, O'Mara had used Fletcher's title of ship commander rather than his Monitor Corps rank of major, Conway noted. It was probably the Chief Psychologist's way of reminding everyone that Fletcher, whether they liked it or not, was the man in charge.

Conway was only half-listening to the Captain as Fletcher, in tones reminiscent of a doting parent extolling the virtues of a favorite offspring, began listing the dimensions and performance and search capabilities of his new command.

The image on the briefing screen was familiar to Conway. He had seen the ship, hanging like an enormous white dart, in the Corps docking area, with its outlines blurred by a small forest of extended sensors and open inspection hatches, and surrounded by a shoal of smaller ships in the drab service coloring of the Monitor Corps. It had the configuration and mass of a Federation light cruiser, which was the largest type of Corps vessel capable of aerodynamic maneuvering within a planetary atmosphere. He was visualizing its gleaming white hull and delta wings decorated with the red cross, occuluded sun, yellow leaf and multitudinous other symbols that represented the concept of assistance freely given throughout the Federation.

" . . . The crew will mostly be comprised of physiological classification DBDG," Captain Fletcher was saying, "which means that they, like the majority of Monitor Corps personnel, are Earth-human or natives of Earth-seeded planets.

"But this is a Tralthan-built ship, with all the design and structural advantages that implies," he went on enthusiastically, "and we have named it the *Rhabwar,* after one of the great figures of Tralthan medical history. The accommodation for extraterrestrial medical personnel is flexible in regard to gravity, pressure, and atmospheric composition, food, furniture and fittings, providing they are warm-blooded oxygen-breathers. Neither the Kelgian DBLF physiological classification" —he looked at Naydrad, then up towards Prilicla— "nor the Cinrusskin GLNO will pose any life-support problems.

"The only physiologically non-specialized section of

the ship is the Casualty Deck and associated ward compartment," Fletcher continued. "It is large enough to take an e-t casualty up to the mass of a fully grown Chalder. The ward compartment has gravity control in half-G settings from zero to five, provision for the supply of a variety of gaseous and liquid atmospheres, and both material and non-material forms of restraint —straps and pressor beams, that is—should the casualty be confused, aggressive or require immobilization for medical examination or surgery. This compartment will be the exclusive responsibility of the medical personnel, who will prepare a compatible environment for and initiate treatment of the casualties I shall bring them.

"I must stress this point," the Captain went on, his tone hardening. "The responsibility for general ship management, for finding the distressed alien vessel and for the rescue itself is mine. The rescue of an extraterrestrial from a completely strange and damaged ship is no easy matter. There is the possibility of activating, by accident, alien mechanisms with unknown potentialities for destruction or injury to the rescuers, toxic or explosive atmospheres, radiation, the often complex problems associated with merely entering the alien ship and the tricky job of finding and bringing out the extraterrestrial casualty without killing it or seriously compounding its injuries . . . "

Fletcher hesitated and looked around him. Prilicla was beginning to shake in the invisible wind of emotional radiation emanating from Naydrad, whose silvery fur was twisting itself into spikes. Murchison was trying to remain expressionless, without much success, and Conway did not think he was being particularly poker-faced, either.

O'Mara shook his head slowly. "Captain, not only have you been telling the medical team to mind their own business, you have been trying to tell them their business. Senior Physician Conway, in addition to his e-t surgical and medical experience, has been involved in a number of ship rescue incidents, as have Pathologist Murchison and Doctor Prilicla, and Charge Nurse Naydrad has specialized in heavy rescue for the past six years. This project calls for close co-operation. You will need the co-operation of your medics, and I strongly suspect that you will get it whether you ask for it or not."

He turned his attention to Conway. "Doctor, you have been chosen by me for this project because of your ability to work with and understand e-ts, both as colleagues and patients. You should encounter no insurmountable difficulties in learning to understand and work with a newly appointed ship commander who is understandably—"

The attention signal on his desk began flashing, and the voice of one of his assistants filled the room. "Diagnostician Thornnastor is here, sir."

"Three minutes," said O'Mara. With his eyes still on Conway he went on: "I'll be brief. Normally I would not give any of you the option of refusing an assignment, but this one is more in the nature of a shakedown cruise for the *Rhabwar* than a mission calling for your professional expertise. We have received distress signals from the scoutship *Tenelphi,* which is crewed exclusively by Earth-human DBDGs, so there won't even be a communications problem. It is a simple search-and-rescue mission, and any charge of incompetence which may be brought against the survivors later will be a Corps disciplinary matter and is not your concern. The *Rhabwar* will be ready to leave in less than an hour. The available information on the incident is on this tape. Study it when you are aboard.

"That is all," he concluded, "except that there is no need for Prilicla or Naydrad to go along just to treat a few DBDG fractures or decompressions. There will be no juicy extraterrestrial cases on *this* trip—"

He broke off because Prilicla was beginning to tremble and Naydrad's fur was becoming agitated. The empath spoke first: "I will, of course, remain in the hospital if requested to do so," Prilicla said timidly, "but if I were to be given a choice, then I would prefer to go with—"

"To us," said Naydrad loudly, "Earth-human DBDGs *are* juicy extraterrestrials."

O'Mara sighed. "A predictable reaction, I suppose.

Very well, you may all go. Ask Thornnastor to come in as you leave."

When they were in the corridor, Conway stood for a moment, working out the fastest, but not necessarily the most comfortable, route for reaching the ambulance ship docking bay on Level 83, then moved off quickly. Prilicla kept pace along the ceiling, Naydrad undulated rapidly behind him and Murchison brought up the rear with the Captain, who was all too plainly afraid of losing his medical team and himself.

Conway's senior physician's armband cleared the way as far as nurses and subordinate grades of doctor were concerned, but there were continual encounters with the lordly and multiply absentminded diagnosticians—who ploughed their way through everybody and everything regardless—and with junior members of the staff who happened to belong to a more heavily muscled species. Tralthans of physiological classification FGLI—warm-blooded oxygen-breathers resembling low-slung, six-legged and tentacled elephants—bore down on them and swept past with the mass and momentum of organic ground vehicles; they were jostled by a pair of ELNTs from Melf, who chittered at them reproachfully despite being outranked by three grades; and Conway certainly did not feel like pulling rank on the TLTU intern who breathed superheated steam and whose protective suit was a great, clanking juggernaut that hissed continually as if it was about to spring a leak.

At the next transection lock they donned lightweight protective suits and let themselves into the foggy yellow world of the chlorine-breathing Illensans. Here the corridors were crowded with the spiny, membranous and unprotected Illensan PVSJs, and it was the oxygen-breathing Tralthans, Kelgians and Earth-humans who wore, or in some cases drove, life-suits. The next leg of the journey took them through the vast tanks where the thirty-foot-long, water-breathing entities of Chalderescol swam ponderously, like armor-plated and tentacled crocodiles, through their warm, green wards. The same protective suits served them here, and although the traffic was less dense, the necessity of having to swim instead of walk slowed them down somewhat. Despite all the obstacles, they finally arrived in the ambulance bay, their suits still streaming Chalder water, just thirty-five minutes after leaving O'Mara's office.

As they boarded the *Rhabwar* the personnel lock swung closed behind them. The Captain hurried to the ship's gravity-free central well and began pulling himself forward towards Control. In more leisurely fashion, the medical team headed for the Casualty Deck amidships. In the ward compartment they spent a few minutes converting the highly unspecialized accommodation and equipment—which were capable of serving the operative and after-care needs of casualties belonging to any of the sixty-odd intelligent life-forms known to the Galactic Federation—into the relatively simple bedding and life-support required for ordinary DBDG Earth-human fracture and/or decompression cases.

Even though the casualties' stay in the ambulance ship would be a matter of hours rather than days, the treatment available during the first few minutes could make all the difference between a casualty who survived and one who was dead on arrival. Even Sector General could do nothing about the latter category, Conway thought; he wondered if any other preparations could be made to receive casualties whose number and condition were as yet unknown.

He must have been wondering aloud, because Naydrad said suddenly, "There is provision for twelve casualties, Doctor, assuming that each member of the scoutship's ten-man crew is injured, and further assuming that two of our crew-members are injured during the rescue, which is a very low probability. Eight of the beds have been prepared for multiple-fracture cases, and the other four for cranial and mandible fractures with associated brain damage necessitating a cardiac or respiratory assist. Self-shaping splints, body restraints and medication suited to the DBDG classification are readily available. When may we learn the contents of O'Mara's tape?"

"Soon, I hope," Conway replied. "Though I lack

the empathic faculty of Prilicla, I feel sure our Captain would not be pleased if we were to discover and discuss the details of our mission without him."

"Correct, friend Conway," said Prilicla. "However, the combination of observation, deduction and experience can in many cases give a non-empathic species the ability to detect or to accurately predict emotional output."

"Obviously," said Naydrad. "But unless someone has something important to say, I shall go to sleep."

"And I," said Murchison, "shall press my not-unattractive face against a viewport and watch. It must be three years since I had a chance to see outside the hospital."

While the Kelgian charge nurse curled itself into a furry question mark on one of the beds, Murchison, Prilicla and Conway moved to a viewport, which at that moment showed only a featureless expanse of metal plating and the foreshortened cylinder of one of the hydraulic docking booms. But as they watched they felt a series of tiny shocks, which were being transmitted through the fabric of the ship. The hospital's outer skin began moving away from them, and the docking boom became even more foreshortened as it came smoothly to full extension, simultaneously releasing the ship and pushing it away.

The distance increased, allowing more and more details to crawl into the port's field of vision—the personnel and stores loading tubes, which were already being withdrawn into their housing; the flashing or steadily burning approach and docking beacons; a line of ports ablaze with the greenish yellow lighting characteristic of the Illensan chlorine-breathers; and a big supply tender sidling up to its docking boom.

Suddenly the picture began to unroll from the top to the bottom of the viewport as the *Rhabwar* applied thrust. It was a gentle, cautious maneuver aimed at placing the ship on a spiral course that would take it through the local hospital traffic to a distance where full thrust could be applied without inconveniencing other ships in the area or elevating the temperature of the hospital's skin—something that would be much

more than an inconvenience if behind such a temporary hot spot there was a ward filled with the fragile,
crystalline, ultra-frigid methane life-forms. The picture
continued to shrink until the whole vast hospital structure was framed in the port, turning slowly as the ship
spiraled away; then thrust was applied, and it slipped
out of sight astern.

With the disappearance of the brilliantly lit hospital,
their night vision returned slowly, and they watched,
in a silence broken only by the hissing noises made
by the sleeping Kelgian, while stars began to develop
in the blank blackness outside the port.

The casualty deck speaker clicked and hummed.
*"This is Control. We are proceeding at one Earth-
gravity thrust until Jump-distance is reached, which
will be in forty-six minutes. During this period the
artificial-gravity grids will be deactivated on all decks
for the purposes of system checking and inspection.
Any e-t requiring special gravity settings please check
and activate its personal equipment."*

Conway wondered why the Captain was not covering the Jump-distance at maximum thrust instead of
dawdling along at one-G. He certainly could not Jump
too close to the hospital, because the creation of an
artificial universe that would allow faster-than-light
travel—even a tiny one capable of enclosing the mass
of their ship—would be much more than an inconvenience to Sector General. It could disrupt every
piece of communications and control equipment in the
place, with dire results for patients and staff alike. But
Fletcher did not seem to be reacting with urgency to
what was, after all, a distress call. Was Fletcher being
overly careful with his nice new ship, Conway wondered, or was he proceeding carefully because the distress call had come before the ship was quite ready
for it?

Though Conway's worrying was causing the Cinrusskin to tremble slightly, Prilicla seemed calm. "I check
my gravity nullifiers every hour, since my continued
existence as a living and thinking entity requires it.
But it is nice of the Captain to worry about my safety.
He appears to be an efficient officer and an entity in

whom we can place full trust where the workings of the ship are concerned."

"I was a little worried for a moment," Conway admitted, laughing at the empath's unsubtle attempt at reassurance. "But how did you know I was worried about the ship? Are you becoming a telepath too?"

"No, friend Conway," Prilicla replied. "I was aware of your feeling and had already noted our somewhat leisurely departure, and I wondered if it was the ship or the Captain who was proceeding cautiously."

"Great minds worry alike," said Murchison, turning away from the viewport. "I could eat a horse," she added with feeling.

"I, too, have an urgent requirement for food," said Prilicla. "What is a horse, friend Murchison, and would it agree with my metabolism?"

"Food," said Naydrad, coming awake.

They did not have to mention the fact that if the *Tenelphi* casualties were serious they might not have many opportunities to eat and it was always a good idea to refuel whenever an opportunity offered itself. As well, Conway thought, eating stopped worrying, at least for a while.

"Food," Conway agreed, and he led the way to the central well, which connected the eight habitable levels of the ship.

As he began climbing the connecting ladder against the one-G thrust aft, Conway was remembering the diagram of the ship's deck layout, which had been projected on O'Mara's screen. Level One was Control, Two and Three held the crew and medics' quarters, which were neither large nor overly well supplied with recreational aids, since ambulance ship missions were expected to be of short duration. Level Four housed the dining and recreational areas, and Five contained the stores of non-medical consumables. Six and Seven were the Casualty Deck and its ward, respectively, and Eight was the Power Room. Aft of Eight was a solid plug of shielding, then the two levels that could not be entered without special protective armor: Nine, which housed the hyperdrive generator, and Ten,

which contained the fuel tanks and nuclear-powered
thrusters.

Those thrusters were making Conway climb very
carefully and hold tightly onto the rungs. A fall down
the normally gravity-free well could quickly change
his status from doctor to patient—or even to cadaver.
Murchison was also being careful, but Naydrad, who
had no shortage of legs with which to grip the rungs,
began ruffling its fur with impatience. Prilicla, using its
personal gravity nullifiers, had flown ahead to check
on the food dispensers.

"The selection seems to be rather restricted," it reported when they arrived, "but I think the quality is
better than the hospital food."

"It couldn't be worse," said Naydrad.

Conway quickly began performing major surgery on
a steak and everyone else was using its mouth for a
purpose other than talking when two green-uniformed
legs came into sight as they climbed down from the
deck above. They were followed by a torso and the
features of Captain Fletcher.

"Do you mind if I join you?" he asked stiffly. "I
think we should listen to the *Tenelphi* material as
soon as possible."

"Not at all," Conway replied in the same formal
tone. "Please sit down, Captain."

Normally a Monitor Corps ship commander ate in
the isolation of his cabin, Conway knew, that being
one of the unwritten laws of the service. The *Rhabwar*
was Fletcher's first command and this his first operational mission, and here he was breaking one of those
rules by dining with crew-members who were not even
fellow officers of the Corps. But it was obvious as the
Captain drew his meal from the dispenser that he was
trying very hard to be relaxed and friendly—he was
trying so hard, in fact, that Prilicla's stable hover over
its place at the table became somewhat unsteady.

Murchison smiled at the Captain. "Doctor Prilicla
tells us that eating while in flight aids the Cinrusskin
digestion as well as cools everyone else's soup."

"If my method of ingestion offends you, friend

Fletcher," Prilicla offered timidly, "I am quite capable of eating while at rest."

"I . . . I'm not offended, Doctor." Fletcher smiled stiffly. "I think *fascinated* would better describe my feelings. But will listening to the tape adversely affect anyone's digestion? The playback can certainly wait until you've all finished."

"Talking shop," said Conway in his best clinical manner, "also aids the digestion." He slotted in the tape, and O'Mara's dry, precise voice filled the compartment . . .

The Monitor Corps scoutship *Tenelphi*, which was currently engaged on preliminary survey operations in Sector Nine, had failed to make three successive position reports. The co-ordinates of the star systems assigned to the *Tenelphi* for investigation were known, as was the sequence in which they would be visited; and since the ship had not released a distress beacon, there was no immediate cause for concern over the fate of the missing vessel. The trouble, as so often happened, might turn out to be a simple communications failure rather than anything dramatic.

Stellar activity in the region was well above the norm, with the result that subspace radio communication was extremely difficult. Signals considered to be important—and they had to be very important indeed, because of the power required to penetrate the highly peculiar medium that was hyperspace—were taped and transmitted repeatedly for as long as was thought necessary, and safe, to do so. The transmission process released harmful radiation, which could not be effectively shielded if the signal was prolonged, especially where lightly built scoutships were concerned. The result was that a terse, highly compressed signal riddled with stellar interference was sent to be pieced together, hopefully in its entirety, from fifty or more identical but individually unreadable messages. Position-report signals were brief and therefore safe, and the power drain was relatively light, even for a scoutship.

But the *Tenelphi* had not sent a position report. Instead, it had transmitted a repeated message to the effect that it had detected and later closed with a large derelict that was falling rapidly into the system's sun, with impact estimated in just under eight days. Since none of the system's planets was within the life-spectrum—unless the life concerned was one of the exotic varieties that might be capable of flourishing on semi-molten rock under a small, intensely hot and aging sun—the assumption had been made that the vessel's entry into the system was accidental rather than the result of a planned mission. There was evidence of residual power remaining in the derelict, and of several pockets of atmosphere of various densities, but no sign of life. The *Tenelphi*'s intention was to board it and investigate.

In spite of the poor signal quality, there could be no doubt of the pleasure felt by the *Tenelphi*'s communications officer at this lucky break in the otherwise deadly monotony of a routine mapping assignment.

" . . . Possibly they became too excited to remember to include a position report," O'Mara's voice continued, "or they knew that the timing of the signal, by checking it against their flight plans, would tell us where they were in general terms. But that was the only coherent message received. Three days later there was another signal, not taped but repeated, each time in slightly different form, by the sender speaking into a microphone. It said that there had been a serious collision, the ship was losing pressure and the crew was incapacitated. There was also some sort of warning. In my professional opinion the voice was distorted by more than the intervening subspace radio interference, but you can decide that for yourselves. Then, two hours later, a distress beacon was released.

"I have included a copy of the second signal, which may help you." The Chief Psychologist's voice added dryly, "Or help confuse you . . . "

Unlike the first signal, the second was virtually unreadable. It was like listening to a mighty storm through which a voice, badly distorted to begin with, was trying to make itself heard in a whisper. They listened intently to the words while trying even harder to ignore the rattling explosions of interstellar static accompanying them, so much so that Naydrad's fur rippled tensely with the strain and Prilicla, who was reacting to everyone else's feelings as well as to the noise, gave up its attempt to hover and settled, trembling, on the table.

" . . . idea if this . . . getting out or . . . crew incap . . . collision with derelict and . . . can't do . . . distress beac . . . work it inside . . . manually . . . but can't assume . . . stupidity of specialization when . . . if signal is getting out . . . warning in case . . . in collision . . . internal pressure dropping . . . can't do anything about that, either . . . how to operate beacon from inside . . . release it manually from . . . al warning in case . . . lets too stiff to . . . confused and not much time . . . only chance is . . . sin chest . . . derelict is close . . . extra suit tanks . . . my specialty . . . ship Tenelphi in collision with . . . crew incapable of any . . . pressure dropping . . . "

The voice went on for several minutes, but the words were lost in a prolonged burst of static. Shortly afterwards the tape ended. There were a few minutes of beautiful silence, during which Naydrad's fur settled down and Prilicla flew up to the ceiling.

"It seems to me that the gist of this message," Conway said thoughtfully, "is that the sender was unsure that the signal was being transmitted, possibly because he was not the communications officer and knew nothing about the equipment he was using, or maybe because he thought the subspace radio antenna had been damaged in the collision, which had, apparently, knocked out the rest of the crew. He did not seem to be able to help them, pressure was dropping, and again due to structural damage, he was unable to release the distress beacon from inside the ship. He would have to have set its timer and pushed it away from the ship with his hands.

"His doubts about the signal going out and his remarks regarding the stupidity of specialization," he went on, "indicate that he was probably not the communications officer or even the Captain, who would have a working knowledge of the equipment in all departments of his ship. The 'lets too stiff' bit could be

'gauntlets too stiff' to operate certain controls or suit
fastenings, and with the ship's internal pressure dropping he might have been afraid to change from his
heavy-duty spacesuit to a lightweight type with its
thinner gauntlets. What an 'al warning' or a 'sin chest'
is, I just don't know, and in any case the distortion
was so bad that those may only be approximations of
the words he used."

Conway looked around the table. "Maybe you can
find something I missed. Shall I play the tape again?"

They listened again, and again, before Naydrad, in
its forthright fashion, told him he was wasting their
time.

"We would know how much credence to place on
the material in this signal," Conway said, "if we knew
which officer sent it and why he, of all the crew, escaped serious injury during the collision. And another
point: Once he says the crew are incapable, and later
he describes them as being incapacitated. Not hurt or
injured, but incapacitated. That choice of word makes
me wonder if he is perhaps the ship's medical officer,
except that he hasn't described the extent of their injuries or, as far as his signal is concerned, done much
to help them."

Naydrad, who was the hospital's expert in ship rescue procedures, made noises like a modulated foghorn,
which translated as, "Regardless of his function in the
ship, there is not much that any officer could do with
fracture and decompression casualties, especially if
everyone was sealed in suits or if the officer himself
was a minor casualty. Regarding the, to me, subtle
difference in meaning between the words *incapacitated*
and *injured,* I think we are wasting time discussing it.
Unless there is a deficiency in this ship's translation
computer that affects only the Kelgian program-
ing . . ."

The Captain bridled visibly at the suggestion that
there might be anything at all wrong with his ship or
its equipment. "This is not Sector General, Charge
Nurse, where the translation computer fills three whole
levels and handles simultaneous translations for six
thousand individuals. The *Rhabwar*'s computer is pro-

gramed only to cover the languages of the ship's personnel, plus the three most widely used languages in the Federation other than our own—Tralthan, Illensan and Melfan. It has been thoroughly tested, and it performs its function without ambiguity, so that any confusion—"

"Undoubtedly lies in the signal itself," Conway contributed hastily, "and not in the translation. But I would still like to know who sent the message. The crew-member who used the words *incapacitated* and *incapable* instead of *hurt* or *injured,* who could not do something because he was confused and short of time and was hampered by gauntlets . . . Dammit, he might at least have told us *something* about the physical condition of the casualties so we'd know what to expect!"

Fletcher relaxed again. "I wonder why he was wearing a suit in the first place. Even if the ship was maneuvering close to the derelict and a collision occurred for whatever reason, it would not have been expected. By that I mean the crew would not normally be wearing spacesuits during such a maneuver. But if they were wearing them, then they were expecting trouble."

"From the derelict?" Murchison asked quietly.

A long silence followed, broken finally by the Captain. "Very unlikely, if it was, in fact, a derelict, and there is no reason to doubt the *Tenelphi's* original report on the situation. If they were not expecting trouble, then we are back with this officer, not necessarily the ship's medic, who was able to get into a spacesuit and perhaps help some of the others into theirs—"

"Without compounding their injuries?" asked Naydrad.

"I can assure you that Monitor Corpsmen are trained to react to situations like this one," said Fletcher sharply.

Reacting to the Captain's growing irritation at the implied criticism of one of his fellow officers, Prilicla joined in: "The broken-up message we received did not mention injuries, so it is possible that the most serious damage is to the scoutship's structure and systems rather than to its crew. *Incapacitated* is not a very strong word. We may find that we have nothing to do."

While approving the little empath's attempt to halt the bickering between Naydrad and the overly touchy ship commander, Conway thought that Prilicla was being far too optimistic. But before anyone could speak there was an interruption.

"Control to Captain. Jump in seven minutes, sir."

Fletcher regarded his half-finished meal for a moment, then stood up. "There is no real need for me to go up there, you know," he said awkwardly. "We took our time coming out to Jump-distance to ensure that the ship was fully operational. It is, in every respect." He gave a short, forced laugh. "But the trouble with good subordinates is that sometimes they make a superior officer feel redundant . . . "

The Captain, Conway thought as Fletcher's legs disappeared up the well, was trying very hard to be human.

Shortly afterwards the ship made the transition into hyperspace, and just under six hours later it reemerged. Because the *Rhabwar* had left the hospital at the end of the medical team's duty period, they had all used the intervening time to catch up on their rest. Nonetheless, there were a few interruptions whenever the Captain relayed what he thought were significant pieces of conversation from Control over the ship's PA system. Obviously, he was simply trying to keep the medics fully informed at every stage of the proceedings. If he had realized the reaction of Conway and the others at being repeatedly awakened to be given information that was either too technically specialized or too elementary, he would have dropped the idea.

Then, suddenly, a relay from Control that signaled the end of any further hope of sleeping for a long time to come.

"We have contact, sir! Two traces, one large and one small. Distance one point six million miles. The small trace matches the mass and dimensions of the Tenelphi.*"*

"Astrogation?"

"Sir. At maximum thrust we can match course,

velocity and position in two hours, seventeen minutes."

"Very well, we'll do that. Power Room?"

"Standing by, sir."

"Four-gravities thrust in thirty seconds, Mr. Chen. Dodds, give Haslam your course figures. Would Senior Physician Conway report to Control as soon as convenient."

Because the physiological classification of the casualties and the general nature of their injuries were already known, it had been decided that Captain Fletcher would remain in the *Rhabwar* while Conway and the other Corps officers boarded the *Tenelphi* to assess the situation. Murchison, Prilicla and Naydrad were standing by on the Casualty Deck, ready to treat the cases as they came through. Since both the casualties and medical team had the same atmosphere and life-support requirements, it was expected that the examination and preliminary treatment time would be short, and that the *Rhabwar* would be returning to Sector General within the hour.

Conway sat in the supernumerary's position in Control, sealed up except for his helmet visor, watching the image of the *Tenelphi* growing larger on the Captain's screen. Flanking the Captain were Haslam and Dodds in the communications and astrogation positions, respectively, also suited except for their gauntlets, which had been removed to facilitate operation of their control consoles. The three officers muttered to one another in the esoteric language of their profession and occasionally exchanged words with Chen, who was in the Power Room aft.

The image of the distressed ship grew until it overflowed the edges of the screen, whereupon magnification was stepped down and it was suddenly tiny again —a bright silver cigar shape tumbling slowly in the blackness, with the immense spherical shape of the derelict turning slowly, like a battered, metal moon, two miles beyond it.

Like Conway, the derelict was being ignored for the present. For no other reason than to register his presence, he said, "It doesn't appear to be too badly damaged, does it?"

"Obviously not a head-on collision," Fletcher responded. "There is serious damage forward, but most of it is to the antennae and sensors, sustained, I think, when she struck and then rolled against the other ship. I can't see the extent of the damage in detail because of the fog. She's still losing a lot of air."

"Which could mean that she still has a lot of air to lose, sir," said Dodds. "Forward tractors and pressors ready."

"Right, check her pitch and roll," ordered the Captain. "But gently. The hull will be weakened, and we don't want to pull it apart. They might not be wearing suits . . . "

He left the sentence hanging as Dodds leaned stiffly over his console. All of the astrogator's attention was concentrated in his fingertips as he focused the immaterial cone-shaped fields of the pressor and tractor beams on the hull of the damaged ship, bringing it slowly and gently to rest with respect to the *Rhabwar*. Seen at rest, the *Tenelphi*'s bow and stern were still obscured by a fog of escaping air, but amidships the vessel seemed to have retained its structural integrity.

"Sir," Haslam reported excitedly, "the midships lock is undamaged. I think we can dock and . . . and walk aboard!"

. . . And evacuate the casualties in a fraction of the time needed for an EVA transfer, Conway thought thankfully. Medical attention was only minutes away for those who had been able to survive thus far. He stood up, closed and sealed his helmet.

"I'll handle the docking," said Fletcher briskly. "You two go with the Doctor. Chen, stay put unless they send for you."

They felt the tiny shock of the *Rhabwar* making contact with the other ship while they were still inside their own midships lock with the inner seal closed behind them. Dodds activated the outer seal, which swung slowly inwards to reveal the outer surface of an identical seal a few inches away. They could see a large, irregular patch of what seemed to be paint or oil, mottled brown and black in color, in the middle of the *Tenelphi*'s seal. The stuff had a ridged, blistered appearance.

"What is that stuff?" Conway asked.

"I haven't a clue," Haslam began, reaching out to touch it. His fingers left yellowish smears and some of the material stuck to his gauntlets. "It's grease, Doctor. The dark color fooled me at first. I expect the heat of the beacon melted and burned off most of it and left the rest looking like that."

"Grease," said Conway. "How did grease get spread over the outer seal?"

Haslam sounded impatient as he replied: "Probably one of the dispenser canisters broke loose during the crash and spun against the seal. There is a pressure nozzle at one end of the canister, which, if depressed with sufficient force, discharges several ounces of grease automatically. If you're very interested, Doctor, I can show you one of them later. Stand back, please, I'm going to open up."

The seal swung open, and Haslam, Conway and Dodds stepped into the *Tenelphi*'s lock chamber. Haslam checked the telltales as Dodds closed the outer seal. The pressure inside the ship was dangerously low, but not lethally low for a person who was fit and healthy. What it would do to an unprotected casualty who might be in shock—with decompression effects accelerating the loss of blood from even superficial cuts and lacerations—was another matter. Suddenly the inner seal opened; their suits creaked and swelled with the pressure differential, and they moved quickly inside.

Haslam gasped. "I don't believe it!"

The lock antechamber was filled with spacesuited figures drifting loosely on the ends of pieces of rope or webbing that had been attached to equipment support brackets or any other convenient tethering point. The emergency lighting system was functioning and bright enough to show all the figures in detail, including the webbing that bound each man's legs together, his arms tightly to his sides and extra air tanks on his back. The spacesuits were all of the rigid, heavy-duty

type, so the tight webbing did not compress the underlying limbs and torsos and whatever injuries they
might have sustained. In each case the helmet visor
was covered by its almost opaque sun filter.

Moving carefully between two of the drifting figures, Conway steadied one and slid back the sun filter. The inside of the visor was badly fogged, but he
could make out a face that was much redder than
normal and eyes that squeezed themselves shut as
soon as the light hit them. He slid back the filter of
another casualty, then another, with similar results.

"Untether them and move them to the Casualty
Deck, quickly," Conway said. "Leave the arm and leg
restraints in place for the present. It makes them easier to move, and the strapping will support the fractured limbs, if any. This is not the complete crew?"

It was not really a question. Obviously, someone
had trussed up the casualties and moved them to the
Tenelphi's airlock to be ready for a fast evacuation.

"Nine here, Doctor," said Haslam after a quick
count. "One crew-member is missing. Shall I look for
him?"

"Not yet," said Conway, thinking that the missing
officer had been a very busy man. He had sent a
subspace radio message, released a distress beacon
when the automatic release mechanism had malfunctioned or he had been unable to work it, and he had
moved his companions from their duty positions in
various parts of their ship to the airlock antechamber.
It was not inconceivable that during these activities
he had damaged his spacesuit and had been forced to
find himself an airtight compartment somewhere to
await rescue.

The man who had accomplished all that, Conway
swore to himself, was damn well going to be rescued!

While he was helping Haslam and Dodds transfer
the first few casualties through to the *Rhabwar,* Conway described the situation for the benefit of those on
the Casualty Deck and for the Captain. Then he
added, "Prilicla, can you be spared back there for a
few minutes?"

"Easily, friend Conway," the little empath replied.

"My musculature is not sufficiently robust to assist directly in the treatment of DBDG casualties. My support is moral rather than medical."

"Fine," said Conway. "Our problem is a missing crew-member who may or may not be injured, perhaps sheltered in an airtight compartment. Will you pinpoint his position for us so we won't waste time searching through wreckage? Are you wearing a pressure envelope?"

"Yes, friend Conway," Prilicla replied. "I'm leaving at once."

It took nearly fifteen minutes for the casualties to be moved out of the *Tenelphi* and into the ambulance ship. By that time Prilicla was drifting back and forth along the exterior of the wreck's hull in an effort to detect the emotional radiation of the missing crew-member. Conway stayed inside the wreck and tried to keep his feelings of impatience and concern under control so as not to distract the Cinrusskin.

If anything lived in the *Tenelphi*, even if it was deeply unconscious or dying, Prilicla's empathic faculty would detect it.

"Nothing, friend Conway," Prilicla reported after twenty interminable minutes. "The only source of emotional radiation inside the wreck is yourself."

Conway's initial reaction was one of angry disbelief.

"I'm sorry, friend Conway," Prilicla replied. "If the being is still in the ship it . . . it is dead."

But Conway had never been one to give up easily on a patient. "Captain, Conway here. Is it possible that he's adrift? Perhaps injured or with his suit radio damaged as a result of releasing the beacon?"

"Sorry, Doctor," Fletcher replied. "We made a radar sweep of the area when we arrived in case the man had accidentally released himself along with the beacon. There is some loose metallic wreckage but nothing large enough to be a man. Nonetheless, I'll make another sweep to be absolutely sure." He paused for a moment, then went on: "Haslam, Dodds. Providing you will not be interfering with the medical treatment down there, check the ID tags and uniform insignias of the casualties and bring me a list. Quickly.

"Chen, you won't be needed in the Power Room for a while," he continued. "Seal up and search the wreck as thoroughly as possible in the time left to us. The casualties are supposed to be moved as quickly as possible to the hospital, and to add to our troubles, this system's sun is coming too close for comfort. You will be looking for the missing officer's body, ship's papers, tapes or anything that might explain what happened here. You should find a crew duty roster attached to the Recreation Deck notice board. By comparing it with the list of casualties, we will be able to tell the identity of the missing man as well as his specialty—"

"I know his specialty," Conway broke in suddenly. He was thinking of the highly professional way in which the missing man had moved the casualties, immobilized them against the possibility of further and perhaps self-inflicted injuries as well as extended the duration of their air supply, and of the amateurish way he had done everything else. "I'm sure he was the ship's medic."

Fletcher did not reply, and Conway began moving slowly around the *Tenelphi*'s lock antechamber. He had the uncomfortable feeling that something should be done, and quickly, but he had no idea what that something was. There was nothing unusual to be seen except, possibly, a wall-mounted clip that was designed to hold three cylindrical canisters about two feet long and that now held only two. Closer inspection showed identification labels on the cylinders, indicating that they contained type GP10/5B grease suitable for use on major actuator mechanisms and control linkages periodically or permanently exposed to low temperature and/or vacuum conditions. Feeling confused and impatient with himself—his job was on the Casualty Deck and not wasting time here—Conway returned to the *Rhabwar*.

Lieutenant Chen was already waiting to enter the lock Conway had just vacated. He opened his visor to speak to the Doctor without tying up the suit frequency and asked Conway if he had been forward to the damaged area of the wreck. Without unsealing his visor Conway shook his head. As Conway moved towards the communication well, Haslam, a piece of folded paper between his teeth to leave both hands free for climbing, came briefly into sight as he pulled himself in the direction of Control. Conway waited until the man had passed, then he stepped into the gravity-free well and began pulling himself aft towards the Casualty Deck.

Of the nine casualties, two of them had already had their spacesuits cut away in small pieces so as not to compound any underlying injuries. Murchison and Dodds were stripping a third without cutting the suit away, and Naydrad was removing the suit of a fourth casualty—also in normal fashion.

Without giving Conway time to ask the inevitable question, Murchison said, "According to Lieutenant Dodds here, all the indications are that these men were already encased in their spacesuits and strapped tightly to their couches *before* the collison occurred. I did not agree at first, but when we stripped the first two and found no injuries, not even bruising . . . ! And the suit fabric was marked by abrasive contact in areas corresponding to the positions of the safety strapping.

"The x-ray scanner lacks definition when used through a spacesuit," she went on, holding the casualty under the arms to steady him while Dodds tugged carefully at the leg sections, "but it is clear enough to show fractures or serious internal injuries. There are none, so I decided that cutting away the suits would be an unnecessary waste of time."

"And of valuable service property," Dodds added with feeling. To a spacegoing Monitor Corps officer, a spacesuit was much more than a piece of equipment, it was analogous to a warm, close-fitting, protective womb. Seeing them being deliberately torn apart would be something of a traumatic experience for him.

"But if they aren't injured," Conway asked, "what the blazes is wrong with them?"

Murchison was working on the man's neck seal

and did not look up. "I don't know," she answered defensively.

"Not even a preliminary diag—"

"No," she said sharply, then went on: "When Doctor Prilicla's empathic faculty established the fact that they were in no immediate danger of dying, we decided that diagnosis and treatment could wait until they were all out of their suits, so our examination thus far has been cursory, to say the least. All I know is that the subspace radio message was correct—they are incapacitated, not injured."

Prilicla, who had been hovering silently over the two stripped patients, joined the conversation timidly. "That is correct, friend Conway. I, too, am puzzled by the condition of these beings. I was expecting gross physical injuries, and instead I find something which resembles an infectious disease. Perhaps you, friend Conway, as a member of the same species, will recognize the symptoms."

"I'm sorry, I did not mean to sound critical," Conway said awkwardly. "I'll help you with that one, Naydrad."

As soon as he took off the man's helmet he could see that his face was red and streaming with perspiration. The temperature was elevated and there was pronounced photophobia, which explained why the glare shields were in place over the visor. The hair was wet and plastered against the man's forehead and skull as if he had just been in for a swim. The drying elements in the suit had been unable to cope with the excessive moisture, so that the interior of the faceplate was opaque with condensation. For that reason Conway did not notice the medication dispenser attached to the collar piece until the helmet had been removed. The medication was in the usual form of an edible transparent plastic tube nipped off at intervals to enclose a single color-coded capsule in each division.

"Did any of the other helmets contain this anti-nausea medication?" asked Conway.

"All of them so far, Doctor," Naydrad replied, its four manipulators working independently on the suit fastenings while its eyes curled up to regard Conway. "The first casualty to be undressed displayed symptoms of nausea when I inadvertently applied pressure to the abdominal region. The being was not fully conscious at the time, so its words were not sufficiently coherent for translation."

Prilicla quickly joined in. "The emotional radiation is characteristic of a being in delirium, friend Conway, probably caused by the elevated temperature. I have also observed erratic, unco-ordinated movements of the limbs and head, which are also symptomatic of delirium."

"I agree," said Conway. But what was causing it? He did not utter the question aloud because he was supposed to know the answer, but he had an uneasy premonition that even a really thorough examination might not reveal the cause. He began helping the charge nurse to remove the patient's sweat-soaked clothing.

There was evidence of heat prostration and dehydration, which, considering the patient's high temperature and associated loss of body fluid, was to be expected. Gentle palpation in the abdominal area caused involuntary retching movements, although there was no foreign material in the stomach so far as Conway could determine. The man had not eaten for more than twenty-four hours.

The pulse was a little fast but steady, respiration irregular and with a tendency towards intermittent coughing. When Conway checked the throat he found it seriously inflamed, and his scanner indicated that the inflammation extended along the bronchi and into the pleural cavity. He checked the tongue and lips for signs of damage by toxic or corrosive material, and noticed that the man's face was not, as he had first thought, wet only with perspiration—the tear ducts were leaking steadily, and there was a mucous discharge from the nose as well. Finally, he checked for evidence of radiation exposure or the inhalation of radioactive material, with negative results.

"Captain. Conway," he called suddenly. "Would you ask Lieutenant Chen, while he is searching the

Tenelphi for the missing officer, to bring back samples of the ship's air and food and liquid consumables? Would he also look for evidence of a leakage of toxic material, solid or gaseous, into the life-support system, and bring them, tightly sealed, to Pathologist Murchison for analysis as quickly as possible?"

"Will do," Fletcher responded. "Chen, you overheard?"

"Yes, sir," said the engineer officer. "I still can't find the missing casualty, Doctor. Now I'm beginning to look in all the unlikely places."

Because Conway's helmet was still sealed, Murchison had been listening to the conversation on the Casualty Deck's speaker as well as hearing his side of it through his suit's external sound system. "Two questions, Doctor," she said irritably. "Do you know what's wrong with them, and has it anything to do with your using that overly loud suit speaker instead of opening your visor and talking normally?"

"I'm not sure," said Conway.

"Perhaps," she said angrily to Dodds, "he doesn't like my perfume."

Conway disregarded the sarcasm and looked around the ward. While he had been examining the casualty with Naydrad, Murchison and Dodds had stripped the others and were obviously waiting for instructions. Prilicla was already carrying out the instructions that Conway had yet to utter on the first two casualties, but then, Prilicla invariably said and did the right thing because it was an exceptionally fine doctor as well as an empath

"If it wasn't for the very high temperature and general severity of their symptoms," Conway said finally, "I'd say we are dealing with a respiratory infection with associated nausea caused, perhaps, by swallowing infected mucus. But the sudden and incapacitating onset of the symptoms makes me doubtful of that diagnosis.

"But that is not the reason I stayed sealed," he went on. "There was no reason for doing so at first. Now, however, I think it would be a good idea if Lieutenant Dodds and you sealed up. It may be an unnecessary precaution."

"Or it may already be too late," said Murchison, unclipping one of the lightweight helmets, which, with its connecting hose, air tank and body webbing, converted the coveralls she was wearing into a protective suit, proof against anything but the most corrosive atmospheres. Dodds had already sealed his visor with remarkable haste.

"Until we can get them to the hospital," Conway said, "treatment must be supportive rather than curative. Replace the lost fluids intravenously, control the nausea and try to keep the temperature down. We may have to use body restraints to keep them from dislodging their monitor leads. Isolate them in pressure tents and raise the oxygen level. I think their condition is going to worsen, and we may eventually need to assist their breathing with a ventilator."

He paused for a moment, and when he looked at Murchison he knew that the concern on his face was concealed by the blurring effect of his visor and by the suit's external speaker, which distorted his voice.

"The isolation may be unnecessary," he said. "These symptoms could just as easily be due to inhaling and swallowing an as yet unidentified toxin. We can't be sure, and we haven't the proper facilities to find the answer in the limited time available. As soon as we find out what happened to the missing crew-man, we'll whisk them all back to Sector General and submit ourselves to a thorough—"

"While we are waiting," Murchison broke in, her voice and features now also distorted by a helmet, "I would like to try to discover what it was that hit them, and what it is that may hit everyone else but yourself."

"There may not be time for that," Conway began, but the voice of the engineer officer reporting to the Captain made him break off.

"Captain, Chen here. I've found the duty roster, sir, and I've checked it against the IDs of the casualties. The missing man turns out to be Surgeon-Lieutenant Sutherland, so the Doctor's guess was

right. But his body is not here. I've searched thoroughly and he's not inside the wreck. There are things missing as well—the ship's portable sound and vision recorders, the crew's personal recorders, cameras, baggage containers, all missing. Clothing and personal effects are drifting about inside the crew's quarters as if they'd been scattered during a hurried unpacking.

"Practically all the spare air tanks have gone, and the equipment register shows that the crew's spacesuits were all logged out for a period of between two and three days, except for the Surgeon-Lieutenant's suit, which wasn't logged out and is missing. The ship's portable airlock is missing also.

"The Control area is badly damaged, so I can't be absolutely sure, but it looks as if they were trying to set up for an automatic Jump, and the instrument settings in the Power Room, which wasn't damaged, supports this. I'd say they were trying to move away from the derelict because of the distortion such a large mass of metal would introduce into the Jump calculations, but they collided with it instead."

"I have the samples for Pathologist Murchison. Shall I come back now, sir?"

"Right away," the Captain ordered.

While Lieutenant Chen and the Captain had been talking, Conway had been trying to make sense out of the strange behavior of the *Tenelphi's* medical officer. Surgeon-Lieutenant Sutherland had displayed professional competence of a very high order in his treatment of the casualties. Through no fault of his own, he had not been able to communicate properly via the subspace radio although he had made a good try, but he had managed to perform the tricky job of manually releasing and activating the distress beacon. It seemed to Conway that Sutherland was a sensible and resourceful officer of the kind who did not panic easily. Neither was he the kind who would get himself killed accidentally or go without leaving some sort of message.

"If he isn't adrift and he isn't on the *Tenelphi,*" said Conway suddenly, "there is only one other place he can be. Can you land me on the derelict, Captain?"

Knowing Fletcher's concern for his ship, Conway expected anything from a flat negative to a verbal explosion at the very suggestion. Instead, he received the kind of response an instructor gives to a pupil of mediocre intelligence—a lecture couched in such elementary language that if the Captain had not been five levels forward in Control, Conway would have risked unsealing his visor to spit in Fletcher's eye.

"I can conceive of no reason, Doctor, why the missing officer should leave the *Tenelphi* when the obvious course would be to stay with the other casualties and await rescue," the Captain began. Then he went on to remind Conway that they did not have a lot of time to waste. Not only should the casualties be hospitalized quickly, but the derelict, the *Tenelphi* and their own vessel were closing with the system's sun at an accelerating rate, which would make it uncomfortably warm for all concerned in two days and would cause their hull to melt in four. There was also the fact that the closer they approached the sun, the more difficult it would be for them to make a Jump.

An added complication was that the *Tenelphi* and the *Rhabwar* were now docked and coupled fore and aft so that the ambulance ship could expand its hyperspace envelope to enclose the wreck, which would have to be taken back with them as evidence in the forthcoming investigation into the collision. With the two ships locked together and only one capable of exerting controlled thrust, delicate maneuvering of the order needed to land him on the derelict would be impossible. If Fletcher attempted it, the *Rhabwar* might well end up in the same condition as the *Tenelphi*. And then there was the sheer size of the derelict . . .

"The vessel is, or was originally, spherical," the Captain went on, and the image from the *Rhabwar*'s telescope appeared on the Casualty Deck's repeater screen. "It is four hundred meters in diameter, with residual power and pressure in a few compartments deep inside the ship. But the *Tenelphi* has already reported the absence of life on board—"

"Sutherland may be on board now, Captain."

Fletcher's sigh made rustling noises on the intercom; then he went on in his patient, lecturing and infuriating voice. "The other ship's findings are more dependable than ours, Doctor. A life indication is the result of a large number of sensor readings comprising the type and distribution of power sources, vibration associated with the mechanical aspects of life-support systems, pressure and temperature variations within the hull, detection of communication or lighting systems, and many more subtle indications. We both realize that many e-ts require ultra-low temperatures or do not see on our visual frequencies, but if anything, they are easier to detect as far as their life-support requirements are concerned.

"But right now," the Captain continued, "I could not say with certainty whether or not anyone or anything was alive inside that thing. The close approach to the sun has heated up the outer hull to such an extent that it is no longer possible to detect subtle differences of temperature inside, and the other sensor readings are badly distorted because of the effect of the heat expansion on the structure as a whole. Besides, that ship is big. Its hull is so torn and punctured by meteorite collisons that Sutherland could have found a way in anywhere. Where would you start looking for him, Doctor?"

"If he's there," said Conway, "he'll let us know where to look."

The Captain remained silent for a moment, and Conway, despite his irritation with Fletcher's manner towards him, could sympathize with the other's dilemma. No more than Conway did the Captain want to leave the area without finding or otherwise establishing the fate of the missing Surgeon-Lieutenant. But there was the welfare of the other casualties to consider, which properly was Conway's responsibility, and the safety of the ambulance ship, which was very definitely Fletcher's.

With all three vessels sliding down the gravity well of the system's sun with an acceleration that did not bear thinking about, the time allocated for a search for the missing officer would be strictly limited, and the Captain would not want to be placed in the position of having to abandon Senior Physician Conway of Sector General as well as the Monitor Corps medic on the derelict. Neither could he risk sending one of his officers with Conway because if he, too, was lost the Captain would have a very serious problem. The *Rhabwar*'s crew was small and there was no overlapping of specialties. Fletcher would probably be able to Jump back to Sector General eventually, but serious risks and delays would be involved that could adversely affect the casualties.

The wall speaker rustled with another sigh, and Fletcher said, "Very well, Doctor, you may search for the Surgeon-Lieutenant. Dodds, take the scope. You are searching for evidence of a recent entry into the derelict. Lieutenant Chen, forget the pathologist's samples for the time being and return to the Power Room. I want maneuvering thrust in five minutes. Doctor, I shall circle the derelict longitudinally at a distance of half a mile. Since it is rotating once every fifty-two minutes, this will enable us to scan its hull surface in four orbits. Haslam, do what you can with the sensors, and give the doctor some idea of the geography of the interior."

"Thank you," said Conway.

Dodds had been helping Murchison move one of the casualties into a pressure tent. As soon as he was finished he excused himself and headed for Control. Conway looked at the repeater screen and the image of the derelict, half of which was a featureless blackness and half a confusion of brilliantly reflective hull plating that was crisscrossed by black fissures and craters. He glanced at it from time to time while he was helping attach bio-sensors to the casualties, seeing it grow larger and begin to unroll from top to bottom of the screen. Suddenly the image flicked off, to be replaced by a diagrammatic representation of the derelict.

It showed the cross section of the spherical vessel, with its deck levels making concentric circles to its core. Near the center several compartments of different sizes were marked in various shades of green, and close to the inner wall of the hull at one point there was a large, rectangular compartment marked in red. Fine red lines joined this area with the green compartments at the center.

"Doctor, Haslam here. I'm projecting a sensor diagram of the derelict's interior. It is not detailed, I'm afraid, and a lot of it is guesswork . . . "

The derelict had been a generation transport, Haslam went on to explain, of the spherical configuration favored at a time when maximum living and cultivating space was a necessity. Direction of travel was along the vertical axis, with the control area forward and the reactor and drive units, which were marked in red, astern. The vessel could rotate fairly rapidly around the vertical axis so as to furnish the outer deck levels amidships with artificial gravity even when the ship was using thrust.

Haslam did not know whether it was one catastrophe or a number of them that had overtaken the ship, but whatever it was it had devastated the control area along with the rest of the outer hull and deck levels and in the process had checked the spin to a fraction of what it should have been. Heavy shielding around the reactors had protected them from serious damage.

The ship had virtually been depopulated, but a number of compartments deep inside the vessel had retained pressure and power, and a number of survivors must have been able to live in them for a time. These were the sections marked in green. The atmosphere inside some of these compartments was little more than a soft vacuum, Haslam added, but in others it was probably still breathable by the present-day members of the species who had built the ship, whoever and whatever they were.

"Is there any possibility . . . ?"

"No survivors, Doctor," Haslam stated firmly. "The *Tenelphi* reported the ship lifeless, derelict. The catastrophe probably happened centuries ago, and the survivors survived for only a short time."

"Yes, of course," said Conway. Then why would Sutherland go there?

"Captain. Dodds. I think I've found something, sir. Just coming into sunlight now. There it is on full magnification."

The repeater screen showed a small area of the derelict's ravaged outer hull. There was a black, jagged-edged opening leading into the depths of the ship, and beside it a section of buckled plating on which there was a large, brownish yellow smear.

"It looks like grease, sir," said Dodds.

"I agree," said the Captain, then impatiently: "But why would he use grease instead of fluorescent green marker paint?"

"Perhaps the stuff was handy, sir."

Fletcher ignored Dodds' reply—it had been a rhetorical question anyway. "Chen, we shall be closing with the derelict to one hundred meters. Haslam, stand by the pressors in case I miscalculate and blunder into that thing. Doctor, under the circumstances I'm afraid I cannot spare an officer to go with you, but a hundred meter flight should pose no serious problems. Just don't spend too much time in there."

"I understand," said Conway.

"Very well, Doctor. Be ready to go in fifteen minutes. Take extra air tanks, water and whatever medical supplies you consider necessary. I hope you find him. Good luck."

"Thank you," said Conway. He wondered what type of medication would be needed for a doctor who seemed to be physically fit but mentally deranged enough to go exploring in the derelict. Regarding his own requirements, he was less hesitant—he would simply increase the duration of his suit to forty-eight hours, at the end of which time the *Rhabwar* would depart, whether he found Sutherland or not.

While Conway was checking the extra tanks, Prilicla flew over and landed on the wall beside him. As they clung to the white plastic surface, the little empath's legs trembled as if it was being subjected to intense emotional radiation. When it spoke Conway was surprised to discover that the emotion was self-generated. It was frightened.

"If I might offer a suggestion, friend Conway," said Prilicla, "the job of finding the being Sutherland would be accomplished much more simply and quickly if I were to accompany you."

Conway thought of the tangle of metal plating and structural members that lay beneath the hull of the derelict, of the danger of rupturing their spacesuits practically every foot of the way, and of the other dangers they could not even guess at. He wondered what had become of the celebrated Cinrusskin cowardice, which in that incredibly fragile species was its most important survival characteristic.

"You would come with me?" Conway asked incredulously. "You are *offering* to come with me?"

Prilicla responded timidly. "Your emotional radiation is somewhat confused, friend Conway, but on the whole flattering to myself. Yes, I shall go with you and use my empathic faculty to help find Sutherland, if he is still alive. However, you already know that I am not a brave person, and I reserve the right to withdraw from the search should the element of risk pass beyond what I consider acceptable limits."

"I'm relieved," said Conway. "For a moment there I was worried about your sanity."

"I know," said Prilicla, beginning to add items to its own spacesuit.

They exited by the small personnel lock forward, the main one being connected to the *Tenelphi,* and had to listen to Captain Fletcher worrying out loud about the situation for several interminable minutes. Then they were outside, and the hull of the derelict was spread out ahead and all around them like a gigantic wall, so pitted and torn and ruptured by centuries of meteorite collisions that at close range the spherical shape of the enormous vessel was not apparent. As they guided themselves towards it, there was a sudden dizzying change of perspective. The derelict was no longer a vertical wall but a vast, metallic landscape on which they were about to touch down, and the two coupled ships were hanging in the sky above it.

Conway found it much easier to guide himself down to the marked area than to control his emotions at the thought of landing on one of the legendary generation ships. But it was likely that his emotional radiation would not inconvenience Prilicla too much because the empath's feelings would be very similar —even though it was physiologically impossible for a Cinrusskin to experience goose bumps or to have the non-existent hair at the back of its neck prickle with sheer wonder.

This was one of the generation ships which, before the discovery of hyperdrive, had carried colonists from their home worlds to the planets of other stars. All of the technologically advanced species of what was now the Galactic Federation had gone through their generation-ship phase. Melf, Illensa, Traltha, Kelgia and Earth had been among the scores of cultures which—between the time of their developing chemical- or nuclear-powered interplanetary travel and virtually instantaneous interstellar flight via the hyperdimension—had flung these planetary seed pods into space.

When a few decades or centuries later the cultures concerned had perfected hyperdrive or received it from one of the species of the emerging Galactic Federation, they had gone looking for these lumbering sub-light-speed behemoths and had rescued the majority of them a few decades or centuries after they had been launched.

This could be accomplished because the courses of the generation ships were known with accuracy, and their positions at any time during their centuries-long voyages could be computed with ease. Provided no physical or psychological catastrophe had occurred in the meantime—and some of the non-physical things that had gone wrong in the generation ships had given the would-be rescuers nightmares for the rest of their lives—the colonists were transferred to their target worlds within a matter of days rather than centuries.

Conway knew that the last of the generation ships to be contacted had been cleared, their metal and reactors salvaged. A few of them had been converted for use as accommodation for personnel engaged on space construction projects more than six hundred years ago. But this particular generation ship was one of the few which had not been contacted when hyperdrive was perfected. Either by accident or because of faulty design, it had gone off course to become a seedling destined never to reach fallow ground.

In silence they landed on the derelict's hull. Because of the vessel's slow spin, Conway had to use his feet and wrist magnets to keep from being tossed gently away again, while Prilicla used its gravity nullifiers in combination with magnetic pads on the ends of its six pipe-stem legs. Carefully they climbed through the gap in the plating and out of the direct sunlight. Conway waited until his eyes adjusted to the darkness, then he switched on his suit spotlight.

There was an irregular natural tunnel in the wreckage, leading down for perhaps thirty meters. At the bottom was a projecting piece of metal, which had been daubed with luminescent green marker paint and a smear of grease.

"If the Tenelphi's *officers marked a route for you,"* Fletcher said when Conway reported the find, *"it should speed the search for Sutherland. Always provided he hasn't been diverted from the marked path. But there is another problem, Doctor. The farther you go into the derelict, the more difficult it will be to work your radio signals. We have more power here than you have in your suit power pack, so you will be able to listen to us long after we will cease hearing you. I'm referring to spoken messages, you understand. If you switch on your radio deep inside the ship, we will still be able to hear it, as a hiss or a burst of static, and vice versa. So even if we can no longer talk to each other, switch on your radio every fifteen minutes to let us know you're still alive, and we'll acknowledge.*

"It is possible to send messages by short and long bursts of static. It is a very old method of signaling

*still used in certain emergency situations. Do you
know Morse?"*

"No," said Conway. "At least, only enough to send
SOS."

"I hope you don't have to, Doctor."

Following the marked path through the wreckage
was slow, dangerous work. The residual spin on the
derelict made them feel as if they were climbing up
towards the center of the ship, while Conway's eyes
and all of his instincts insisted that he was moving
downwards. When they reached the first daub of
paint and grease, another mark became visible
deeper inside the ship, but the path inclined sharply
to avoid a solid mass of wreckage and the next leg of
the journey angled in a new direction for the same
reason. They were progressing towards the center of
the ship, but in a series of flat zigzags.

Prilicla had taken the lead to avoid the risk of
Conway falling onto it. With its six legs projecting
through its spherical pressure envelope—Prilicla's
bony extremities were not affected by vacuum conditions—it looked like a fat metallic spider picking its
way gracefully through a vast, alien web. Only once
did its magnetic pads slip, when it began to fall towards him. Instinctively, Conway reached out a hand
to check the creature's slow tumble as it was going
past, then pulled his hand back again. If he had
gripped one of those fragile legs, it would probably
have snapped off.

But Prilicla checked its own fall with the suit
thrusters, and they resumed the long, slow climb.

Just before communications with the ambulance
ship became unworkable, Fletcher reported that they
had been gone four hours, and asked if Conway was
sure that he was following the missing Sutherland and
not just the path marked by the party of the *Tenelphi*
crew-members. Conway looked at the patch of luminous paint just ahead of them, and at the smear of
grease beside it, and said he was sure.

I'm missing something, he told himself angrily,
something that is right in front of my stupid face . . . !

As they moved deeper into the ship the wreckage

became less densely packed, but the apparent gravity pull exerted by the spin had diminished so much that quite large masses of plating, loose equipment and demolished furnishings moved or slipped or settled ponderously whenever they tried to grip them. The suit spotlights showed other things, too—crushed, torn and unidentifiable masses of desiccated organic material, which were the remains of the crew or domestic animals caught in the centuries-old catastrophe. But separating the organic from the metallic wreckage would have been both highly dangerous and a waste of time. Finding Sutherland had to take priority over satisfying their curiosity regarding the physiological classification of the species that had built the ship.

They had been traveling for just under seven hours and had begun to move through levels that, although their structure was ruptured and contorted, were no longer choked with wreckage. This was fortunate because Prilicla kept blundering gently into walls and bulkheads through sheer fatigue, and every second or third breath that Conway took seemed to turn into a yawn.

He called a halt and asked the empath if it could detect any emotional radiation apart from Conway's own. Prilicla said no and was too tired even to sound apologetic. When Conway next heard the periodic hiss in his suit phones, he acknowledged by flipping his transmit switch on and off rapidly three times, pausing, then repeating the signal at short intervals for several minutes.

The Captain would realize, he hoped, that the repeated S signal meant that Prilicla and Conway were going to sleep.

They made much better time on the next stage of the journey, which involved simply walking along virtually undamaged decks and climbing broad ramps or narrower stairs towards the center of the ship. Only once did they have to slow to negotiate a plug of wreckage, which had been caused, apparently, by a large and slow-moving meteorite that had punched its way deep inside the ship. A few minutes later they found their first internal airlock.

Obviously the lock had been built by the survivors after the catastrophe, because it was little more than a large metal cube welded to the surround of an airtight door and containing a very crude outer seal mechanism. Both seals were open and had been that way for a very long time, because the compartment beyond was filled with desiccated vegetation, that practically exploded into dust when they brushed against it.

Conway shivered suddenly as he thought of the vast ship, grievously but not mortally wounded by multiple meteorite collisions, blinded but not powerless, and with groups of survivors living in little islands of light and heat and isolated by steadily dropping pressure. But the survivors had been resourceful. They had built airlocks, which had enabled them to travel between their islands and co-operate in the matter of life-support, and they had been able to go on living for a time.

"Friend Conway," said Prilicla, "your emotional radiation is difficult to analyze."

Conway laughed nervously. "I keep telling myself that I don't believe in ghosts, but I still won't believe me."

They went around the hydroponics room because the markers said that they should, and an hour or so later they entered a corridor that was intact except for two large ragged-edged holes in the ceiling and deck. There was a strange dilution of the absolute darkness of the corridor, and they switched off their spotlights.

A faint glow was coming from one of the holes, and when they moved to the edge it was as if they were looking down a deep well with a tiny circle of sunlight at the bottom. Within a few seconds the sunlight had disappeared, and for a few more seconds the wreckage at the other end of the tunnel was illuminated. Then the darkness was complete again.

"Now," Conway said with relief, "at least we know a shortcut back to the outer hull. But if we hadn't happened to be here at precisely the right time when the sun was shining in—"

He broke off, thinking that they had been very lucky and that there might be more luck to come, because at the end of the corridor containing the newly discovered exit they could see another airlock. It was marked with luminous paint and a very large smear of grease, and the outer seal was closed, a clear indication that there was pressure in the compartment beyond.

Prilicla was trembling with its own excitement as well as with Conway's as Conway began to operate the simple actuator mechanism. He had to stop for a moment because the suit radio was hissing at him and he had to acknowledge. But when he had done so it kept on hissing at him.

"The Captain is not a very patient man," said Conway irritably. "We've been gone just over thirty-eight hours and he said he would give me two days . . . " He paused for a moment and held his breath, listening to the faint, erratic hissing, which was quieter than the sound of his own breathing, so deep inside the derelict had they penetrated. It was difficult to tell when a hiss stopped or started, but gradually he detected a pattern in the signals. Three short bursts. Pause. Three long bursts. Pause. Three short bursts, followed by a longer pause, after which the sequence was repeated again and again. A distress signal. An SOS . . .

"There can't be anything wrong with the ship," he said. "That would be ridiculous. So it has to be a problem with the patients. Anyway, they want us back there and I would say the matter is urgent."

Prilicla, clinging to the wall beside the airlock, did not reply for several seconds. Finally it said, "Pardon the seeming unpoliteness, friend Conway, but my attention was elsewhere. It is at the limit of my range, but I have detected an intelligent life-form."

"Sutherland!" said Conway.

"I should think so, friend Conway," Prilicla said. It began to tremble in sympathy with Conway's dilemma.

Somewhere within a few hundred feet was the missing *Tenelphi* medic, physical condition unknown, but very definitely alive. It might take an hour or more to find him, even with Prilicla's help. Conway desperately wanted to find and rescue the man, not just for the usual reasons but because he felt sure that he possessed the answer to what had happened to the other *Tenelphi* officers. But he and Prilicla were wanted back on the *Rhabwar,* urgently. Fletcher would not send an SOS signal without good reason.

Obviously the ship was not in distress, so it had to be a problem involving the patients. A sudden worsening of their condition, perhaps, which was serious enough for Murchison and Naydrad—two beings who did not panic without reason—to agree to this method of recalling the two doctors. But, thought Conway suddenly, one doctor could satisfy them temporarily until they got two more a little later, one of whom, Sutherland, had a greater knowledge of the malady concerned than the ambulance ship medics.

Prilicla ceased trembling as soon as Conway made his decision. He turned to his companion. "Doctor, we'll have to split up. They need us urgently on the ship, or maybe they just want to talk to us urgently. Would you mind taking the shortcut to the outer hull? Find out what the problem is and give what advice you can. But don't move away from the outer end of that tunnel for at least an hour after you get there. If you do that you will be in line of sight with the *Rhabwar* and, via the tunnel, with me down here, and can relay messages in either direction.

"You should be able to get to the other end of the tunnel, with no zigzagging necessary and with the centrifugal force of the spin helping you along, in roughly two hours," Conway went on. "This should give me enough time to find Sutherland and start bringing him out. It has to be my job because it will need DBDG muscles rather than Cinrusskin sympathy to help him through that tunnel."

"I agree, friend Conway," said Prilicla, already moving along the corridor towards the opening. "I

have rarely agreed to a request with more enthusiasm . . . "

The first surprise when he went through the airlock
was that there was light. He found himself in a large,
open compartment, which, judging from the remains
of equipment attached to the deck, walls and ceiling,
had been the ship's assembly and recreation area. The
equipment, which had originally been used for weightless exercising and probably for competitive sports
as well, had been drastically modified to provide supports for the sandwich hammocks, which were necessary for sleeping in the weightless condition. Apart
from a few sections sheeted in with transparent plastic
and containing vegetation, some of which was still
green, the interior surfaces of the enormous compartment were covered with bedding and furniture
modified for gravity-free conditions. It looked as if
up to two hundred survivors of the original meteorite
collisions, including their young, had once been
packed into this compartment. The visual evidence
indicated that they had lived there for a long time.
The second surprise was that there were no traces of
them other than the furniture and fittings they had used.
Where were the bodies of the long-dead survivors?

Conway felt his scalp prickle. He turned up the
volume of his external suit speaker to full and yelled
"Sutherland!"

No response.

Conway launched himself across the compartment
towards the opposite wall, where there were two
doors. One of them was partly open and light was
shining through. When he landed beside it he knew it
was the ship's library.

It was not just the neat racks of books and tape-
spools that covered the walls and ceiling of the empty
room, or the reading and scanning equipment attached to the deck, or even the present-day tapes and
portable recorders that had belonged to the *Tenelphi*
officers but that had been abandoned to drift weightlessly about the room. He knew it was the library
because he had been able to read the sign on the
door, just as he was able to read the name below the

ship's crest mounted at eye-level on the opposite wall. As he stared at that famous crest everything suddenly became clear.

He knew why the *Tenelphi* had run into trouble, why the officers had left their ship for the derelict, leaving only their medic as watch-keeping officer. He knew why they had returned so hastily, why they were sick and why there was so little he, or anyone else for that matter, could do for them. He also knew why Surgeon-Lieutenant Sutherland used grease instead of marker paint, and he had a fair idea of the situation confronting the doctor that had driven him back to the derelict. He knew because that ship's name and crest appeared in the history books of Earth and of every Earth-seeded planet.

Conway swallowed, blinked away the fog that was temporarily impairing his vision, and backed slowly out of the room.

The sign on the other door had read *Sports Equipment Stowage,* but it had been relettered *Sick Bay.* When he slid it open he found that it, too, was lighted, but dimly.

Along the walls on both sides of the door, equipment storage shelves had been modified to serve as tiers of bunks, and two of them were occupied. The bodies occupying them were emaciated to the point of deformity, partly because of malnutrition and partly because of being born and living out their lives in the weightless condition. Unlike the desiccated sections of bodies Prilicla and he had encountered on the outer decks, these two had been exposed to atmosphere, and decomposition had taken place. The process was not sufficiently advanced, however, to conceal the fact that the bodies were of classification DBDG, an old male and a girl-child, both Earth-human, and that their deaths had occurred within the past few months.

Conway thought of the voyage that had lasted nearly seven centuries and of the last two survivors who had almost made it, and he had to blink again. Angrily, he moved deeper into the room, pulling himself along the edge of a treatment table and instrument cabinet. In a far corner his spotlight illuminated a spacesuited figure holding a squarish object in one hand and supporting itself against an open cabinet door with the other.

"S . . . Sutherland?"

The figure jerked and in a weak voice replied, "Not so bloody loud."

Conway turned down the volume of his speaker and said quickly, "I'm glad to see you, Doctor. I'm Conway, Sector General. We have to get you back to the ambulance ship quickly. They're having problems there and . . . "

He broke off because Sutherland was refusing to let go of the cabinet. Reassuringly, Conway went on: "I know why you used yellow grease instead of paint, and I haven't unsealed my helmet. We know there is pressure in other parts of the ship. Are there any survivors? And did you find what you were looking for, Doctor?"

Not until they were outside the sick bay with the door closed behind them did Sutherland speak. He opened his visor, rubbed at the moisture beading the inside of it. "Thank God somebody remembers his history," he said weakly. "No, Doctor, there are no survivors. I searched the other air-filled compartments. One of them is a sort of cemetery of inedible remains. I think cannibalism was forced on them at the end, and they had to put their dead somewhere where they would be, well, available. And no again, I didn't find what I was looking for, just a means of identifying but not curing the condition. All the indicated medication spoiled hundreds of years ago . . . " He gestured with the book he was holding. "I had to read some fine print in there, so I increased the air pressure inside my suit so that when I opened my visor for a closer look it would blow away any airborne infection. In theory it should have worked."

Obviously it had not worked. In spite of the higher pressure inside his suit blowing air outwards through his visor opening, the Surgeon-Lieutenant had caught what his fellow officers had. He was sweating profusely, squinting against the light and his eyes were streaming, but he was not delirious or unconscious, as the other officers from the *Tenelphi* had been. Not yet.

"We found a quick way out," Conway said. "Well, relatively. Do you think you can climb with my assistance; or should I tie your arms and legs and lower you ahead of me?"

Sutherland was in poor shape, but he most emphatically did not want to be tied and lowered, no matter how carefully, down a tunnel whose walls were of twisted and jagged-edged metal. They compromised by strapping themselves together back to back, with Conway doing the climbing and the other medic fending them off the obstructions Conway could not see. They made very good time, so much so that they had begun to catch up to Prilicla before the Cinrusskin was more than halfway along the tunnel. Every time the sun shone into the other end, the dark circle that was the empath's spacesuited body seemed larger.

The continuous hissing of the SOS signal grew louder by the minute, then suddenly it stopped.

A few minutes later the tiny black circle that was Prilicla became a shining disk as the empath cleared the mouth of the tunnel and moved into sunlight. It reported that the *Rhabwar* and the *Tenelphi* were in sight, and that there should be no problem making normal radio contact. They heard it calling the *Rhabwar*, and what seemed like ten years later came the hissing and crackling sound of the ambulance ship's reply. Conway was able to make out some of the words through the background mush, so he was not completely surprised by Prilicla's relayed message.

"Friend Conway," said the empath, and he could imagine it trying desperately to find some way of softening the effect of its bad news. "That was Naydrad. All the DBDG Earth-humans on the ship, including Pathologist Murchison, are displaying symptoms similar to those of the *Tenelphi* officers, with varying degrees of incapacity. The Captain and Lieutenant Chen are the least badly affected so far, but both are in a condition that warrants their being confined to bed. Naydrad requires our assistance urgently, and the Captain says he'll leave without us if we don't hurry up. Lieutenant Chen is doubtful about our leaving at all, even if they weren't having to modify the hyperdrive envelope to accommodate the *Tenelphi*. It seems there are additional problems caused by the proximity of the system's sun that require a trained astrogator to—"

"That's enough," Conway broke in sharply. "Tell them to dump the *Tenelphi!* Decouple and undock and jettison any samples Chen took aboard for analysis. Neither Sector General nor the Monitor Corps will thank us for bringing back anything that has been in contact with the derelict. They might not be too happy to see us—"

He broke off as he heard Naydrad's voice relaying his instructions to the Captain and the beginning of Fletcher's reply. He went on quickly: "Prilicla, I'm receiving the ship direct, so I don't need you as a relay anymore. Return to the ship as quickly as possible and help Naydrad with the patients. We should be clear of this tunnel in fifteen minutes. Captain Fletcher, can you hear me?"

A voice which Conway did not recognize as the Captain's said, "I can hear you."

"Right," said Conway, and very briefly he explained what had happened to the *Tenelphi* and themselves . . .

Finding a derelict in the system they were surveying had been a welcome break in the monotony for the scoutship and for the off-duty officers who went on board to investigate and, if possible, identify the vessel. Like all scoutships on survey duty, the *Tenelphi* had a complement consisting of a Captain and his astrogation, communications, engineering and medical officers, while the remaining five were the survey specialists, whose work went on around the clock.

According to Sutherland, the first officers to board the derelict had identified the ship very quickly, because of a lucky find of a store requisition form, dated and headed with the ship's crest. The result had been that everyone, including the Captain, had hastily transshipped to the derelict. The sole exception was the ship's medic, whose specialty was considered the least useful on what had suddenly become a mass information-gathering exercise.

For the derelict was none other than the *Einstein,* the first starship to leave Earth and the only one of those early generation ships from that planet not to be rescued by the later hyperdrive vessels. Many attempts at rescuing it had been made over the centuries, but the *Einstein* had not followed its intended course. It had been assumed that the ship had suffered a catastrophic malfunction within a relatively short time of leaving the solar system.

And now here it was, the first and undoubtedly the bravest attempt by mankind to reach the stars the hard way, because at that time its technology had been untried, because nobody knew with absolute certainty that its target system contained habitable planets, and because its crew, the very best people that Earth could produce, wanted to go anyway. As well, the *Einstein* was a piece of technological and psychosociological history, the embodiment of one of the greatest legends of star travel. Now this great ship with its priceless log and records was falling into the sun and would be destroyed within the week. Small wonder, therefore, that the *Tenelphi* was left with only its medical officer on board. But even he did not realize that there was any danger in the situation until the crew, sick and sweating and near delirium, began to return. From the onset Sutherland had discarded Conway's first assumptions, that their condition was due to radiation poisoning, inhaling toxic material or eating infected food, because the returning officers told him about the conditions on board the derelict and how long some of the descendants of its crew had been able to survive.

Not only did the ship carry priceless records of man's first attempt at interstellar flight, it also contained an unknown quantity and variety of bacteria —preserved by the heat and atmosphere and recently living human organisms—of a type which had existed

seven hundred years ago and for which the human
race no longer had immunity.

Noting the rapidly worsening condition of his fellow officers and knowing there was little he could do
for them, Sutherland insisted that they all wear spacesuits continually to avoid the possibility of cross-
infection—he could not be absolutely sure they were
all suffering from the same disease—and as protection in case of accidents while they were moving clear
of the derelict. Their intention was to Jump to Sector
General, where some high-powered medical assistance would be available.

When the collision—the inevitable collision, according to Sutherland, considering the semi-conscious
and delirious condition of the crew—occurred, he
moved the men to the lock antechamber in preparation for a quick evacuation, tried to send a subspace
radio signal, and not knowing if he was doing the job
properly, tried to eject the distress beacon. But the
collision had damaged the release mechanism, and he
had to push it out of the airlock. His patients' condition was worsening, and he wondered again if there
was anything at all that he could do for them.

It was then that he decided to go aboard the derelict himself, to look for a cure in the very place the
disease had originated. The solution might be in the
derelict's medicine chest, the "sin chest" of the
garbled radio signal. With pressure dropping steadily
aboard the badly damaged *Tenelphi* and all the recorders abandoned on the derelict, he could not leave
a proper warning for any would-be rescuers. But he
had done his best.

He had smeared the *Tenelphi's* airlock outer seal
with yellow grease, not knowing that the heat from
the distress beacon would turn it brown, and he had
marked his path through the derelict in similar fashion.
Few people these days realized, and even Conway
had been slow to remember, that in pre-space-travel
times a ship with disease on board flew a yellow
flag . . .

"Sutherland discovered that the medication in the
Einstein's sick bay had long since spoiled," Conway

went on, "but he did find a medical textbook which mentioned a number of diseases with symptoms similar to those shown by our people. It is one of the old influenza variants, he thinks, although in our case the loss of natural immunity over the centuries means that these symptoms are being experienced with much greater severity, and any prognosis would be uncertain. That is why I would like you to record this information for proper subspace transmission to Sector General, so that they will know exactly what to expect. And I suggest you make preparations for an automatic Jump, in case you aren't feeling well enough to—"

"Doctor," the Captain replied weakly, "I'm trying to do just that. How quickly can you get back here?"

Conway remained silent for a moment while he and Sutherland cleared the edge of the tunnel. "I have you in sight. Ten minutes."

Fifteen minutes later Conway was removing Sutherland's spacesuit and uniform on the Casualty Deck, which was rapidly becoming overcrowded. Doctor Prilicla was hovering over the patients in turn, keeping an eye and an empathic faculty on their condition, while Naydrad brought in Lieutenant Haslam, who had collapsed at his position in Control a few minutes earlier.

Neither of the extraterrestrials had anything to fear from terrestrial pathogens, even seven-hundred-year-old pathogens. The *Tenelphi* and *Rhabwar* crewmembers and Murchison could only lie and hope, if they weren't already delirious or unconscious, that their bodies' defenses would find some way of fighting this enemy from the past. Only Conway had remained free from infection, because a smear of grease or something in a garbled radio signal had worried his subconscious to the extent that he had not unsealed his visor after the scoutship's officers had been brought aboard.

"Four-G thrust in five seconds," came Chen's voice from the speaker. "Artificial gravity compensators ready."

The next time Conway looked at the repeater screen it showed the *Einstein* and the *Tenelphi* shrunk to the size of a tiny double star. He finished making Sutherland as comfortable as possible, checked his IVs and moved on to Haslam and Dodds. He was leaving Murchison to the last, because he wanted to spend more time with her.

She was perspiring profusely despite the reduced temperature inside the pressure litter, muttering to herself and turning her head from side to side, eyes half-open but not really conscious of his presence. He was shocked to see Murchison like this. He realized that she was a very seriously ill patient instead of the colleague he had loved and respected since the days when she was a nurse in the FGLI maternity section, when he was convinced that all the ills of the Galaxy could be cured by his pocket x-ray scanner and his dedication to his profession.

But in Sector General, where the lowliest member of the medical staff would be considered a leading authority in a single-species planetary hospital, all things were possible. An able nurse with wide e-t experience could move up and across the lines of promotion to become one of the hospital's best pathologists, and a junior doctor with unconventional ideas bubbling about in a head that was much too large could learn sense. Conway sighed, wanting to touch and reassure her. But Naydrad had already done all that it was possible to do for her, and there was nothing he could do except watch and wait while her condition deteriorated towards that of the *Tenelphi* officers.

With any luck they would soon be transferred to the hospital, where more high-powered help and resources were available. Fletcher and Chen had been lucky in that the Captain had been in Control and the engineer officer in the Power Room while the infected *Tenelphi* officers were being brought aboard, so they had been the last two to be affected. Fortunately, they were still fit enough to work the ship.

Or were they . . . ?

The repeater screen was still showing an expanse of

blackness in which the *Einstein* and the *Tenelphi* were indistinguishable among the background stars. But by now the screen should be showing the non-color of the hyperdimension. It would be much better for all concerned, Conway thought suddenly, if he stopped doing nothing for Murchison and tried to do something for Chen and the Captain.

"Friend Conway," said Prilicla, indicating with one of its feelers, "would you look at this patient, please, and at the one over there? I feel they are conscious and need reassurance by a member of their own species."

Ten minutes later Conway was in the well, pulling himself towards Control. As he entered he could hear the voices of the Captain and engineer officer calling numbers to each other, with frequent stops for repeats and rechecks. Fletcher's face was red and dripping with perspiration, his eyes were streaming and his delirium seemed to have taken the form of a rigid professional monomania as he blinked and squinted at the displays on his panel and read off the numbers. Meanwhile, Chen, who did not look much better, replied from the strange position of the astrogator's panel. Conway regarded them clinically and did not like what he saw.

"You need help," he said firmly.

Fletcher looked up at him through red-rimmed, streaming eyes. "Yes, Doctor, but not yours. You saw what happened to the *Tenelphi* when the medical officer tried to pilot it. Just tend to your patients and leave us alone."

Chen rubbed sweat from his face. "What the Captain is trying to say, Doctor, is that he can't teach you in a few minutes what it took him five years of intensive training to learn, and that the delay in making the Jump is caused by our having to get it right first time in case we aren't fit enough for a second try and we materialize in the wrong galactic sector, and that he is sorry for his bad manners but he is feeling terrible."

Conway laughed. "I accept his apology. But I have just come from speaking to one of the *Tenelphi* victims of what we now feel sure is one of the old influenza variants. He was one of the first to fall sick along with the other member of the original boarding party. Now his temperature is returning to normal and that of the other one is also falling rapidly. I would say that this outbreak of seven-hundred-year-old flu can be treated successfully with supportive medication, although the hospital will probably insist on a period of quarantine for all of us when we get back.

"However," he went on briskly, "the officer I speak of is the *Tenelphi*'s astrogator, and frankly, he is in much better shape than either of you two. You *do* need help?"

They were looking at him as if he had just produced a miracle, as if in some peculiar fashion Conway was solely responsible for all the complex mechanisms evolved by the DBDG Earth-human lifeform to protect itself against disease—which was, of course, ridiculous. He nodded to them and returned to the Casualty Deck to send up the *Tenelphi* astrogator. He was thinking that within two weeks at most, everyone apart from the immune Prilicla and Naydrad would be fully recovered and convalescent, and he would no longer have to treat Pathologist Murchison as a patient.

PART TWO

Quarantine

Immediately on its return to Sector General, the *Rhabwar* and the Earth-human personnel on board were placed in strict quarantine and refused admission to the hospital. Conway, who had had no direct physical contact with either the *Tenelphi*'s or his ambulance ship's crews since the infection had come aboard, was doubly quarantined in that he inhabited the man-shaped bubble of virus-free air that was his long-duration spacesuit and a cabin hastily modified to provide life-support independent of the ship's infected system.

There was no real problem in providing supportive treatment to both crews—who were either responding well or were in varying stages of convalescence—because he had Prilicla and Naydrad assisting him. As extraterrestrials they were, of course, impervious to Earth-human pathogens, and they were being very smug about this. Neither was there any difficulty in accommodating the two crews—the officers of the *Tenelphi* occupied the Casualty Deck, and the ambulance ship personnel had their own cabins. But there were periods, often as long as twenty-three hours in the day, when the *Rhabwar* was dreadfully overcrowded.

The real problem was that while the hospital refused them admittance, practically every Earth-

human and e-t in Sector General was trying to find an
excuse to visit the ambulance ship.

During the first week, combined medical and engineering teams worked around the clock flushing out
the ship's air system and sterilizing everything with
which the infected air had come in contact. There
were also constant checks on the progress of the
patients and constant supervision of the regimen,
which would ensure that after their cure was effected
they would not retain the ability of passing on the
infection to any other member of the Earth-human
DBDG classification. Lastly, there were those who
came simply to talk to the patients and complain
about Conway's handling of the *Einstein* incident.

These included Thornnastor, the elephantine Tralthan diagnostician in charge of the Pathology Department, who came chiefly to raise the morale of
its department-member Murchison by providing her
with the latest hospital gossip, which in some of the e-t
wards was colorful; and a variegated bunch of highly
professional medics and bitterly disappointed amateur
historians who wanted to talk to the *Tenelphi* crew
about their experiences aboard the derelict, and to
castigate Conway for not bringing back more in the
way of specimens than a seven-hundred-year-old medical textbook, which had fallen apart as soon as it was
exposed to present-day sterilization techniques.

Inside his suit-shaped bubble of sterile air, Conway
tried, not always successfully, to remain emotionally
cool and aloof. Captain Fletcher, whose convalescence had advanced to the stage where he was convinced that medical red tape was all that was keeping
him from resuming active duty, could not remain cool
at all. Especially when the *Rhabwar* personnel
gathered together at mealtimes.

"You are a senior physician, after all, and you are
still the ranking medical officer on this ship," the
Captain observed in an aggrieved tone while he attacked the rather bland meal the hospital dietitians
had prescribed for them. "Unlike us, Doctor, you
never were a patient, so your rank was not taken
away when you were issued a hospital gown. I mean,

Thornnastor is all right as a person, but it's an FGLI, after all, and its movements are about as graceful as those of a six-legged baby elephant. Did you see what it did to the ladder on the Casualty Deck, and to the door of your cabin, ma'am?"

He broke off to smile admiringly at Murchison. Lieutenant Haslam muttered something about often feeling like breaking down the pathologist's door himself, and the Captain silenced him with a frown. Lieutenants Dodds and Chen, like the good junior officers they were, maintained a respectful silence, and in common with the other male Earth-human DBDGs present, exuded minor-key emotional radiation of a pleasurable* nature, which Prilicla would have described as being associated with the urge to reproduce. Charge Nurse Naydrad, who rarely allowed anything to interfere with bodily refueling, kept on moving large portions of the green and yellow vegetable fiber it was pleased to call food, and ignored them.

The emotion-sensitive Doctor Prilicla, who could ignore nobody, hovered silently above the edge of the table, showing no signs of emotional distress. Obviously the Captain was not as irritated as he sounded.

" . . . Seriously, Doctor," Fletcher went on, "it isn't just Thornnastor blundering into areas of the ship that were not meant for FGLIs. Some of the other e-ts take up a lot of space as well, and there are times when each crew-member of the *Tenelphi* has about half a dozen e-ts or Earth-humans sitting at his feet while he chatters on and on about the things he saw on that derelict, and they treat us as if we'd caught a mutated form of leprosy instead of the same influenza virus as the scoutship crew."

Conway laughed. "I can understand their feelings, Captain. They lost material of priceless historic value, which was already considered irretrievably lost for many centuries. That means they have lost it twice and feel twice as angry with me for not bringing back an ambulance shipful of records and artifacts from the *Einstein*. At the time I was tempted. But who knows what else I might have brought back with those records in the way of seven-hundred-year-old bacterial and viral infections from which we have little or no immunity? I couldn't take the risk, and they, when they stop being bitterly disappointed amateur historians and go back to being the hospital's top seniors and diagnosticians, will know that, given the same circumstances, they would have done exactly what I did."

"I agree, Doctor," said Fletcher, "and I sympathize with your problem and theirs. I also know that they have to undergo a very thorough and, well, physically inconvenient decontamination procedure on leaving the ship, regardless of their physiological classifications, and this weeds out all but the most enthusiastic or masochistic amateur historians. All I want to know is whether there is a polite way, or any way, of telling them to stay off my ship."

"Some of them," said Conway helplessly, "are diagnosticians."

"You say that as if it was some kind of answer, Doctor," said the Captain, looking perplexed. "What is so special about a diagnostician?"

Everyone stopped eating to look at Conway, who alone among them could not eat anywhere outside his sterile cabin. Prilicla's hover became somewhat unstable, and Naydrad gave a short foghorn blast that was untranslatable but was probably the Kelgian equivalent of a snort of incredulity.

It was Murchison who finally spoke. "The diagnosticians are very special, Captain," she said. "And peculiar. You already know that they are the top-ranking medical personnel in the hospital, and as such, cannot be readily ordered around. Another reason is that when you speak to one of them you can never be sure who or what you are talking to . . ."

Sector General was equipped to treat every known form of intelligent life, Murchison explained, but no single person could hold in his or its brain even a fraction of the physiological data necessary for this purpose. Surgical dexterity and a certain amount of e-t diagnostic ability came with training and experience, but the complete physiological knowledge of any

patient requiring complex treatment was furnished by
means of an Educator tape. This was simply the brain
recording of some great medical authority belonging
to the same species as or a species similar to that of
the patient undergoing treatment.

If an Earth-human doctor had to treat a Kelgian
patient, he took a DBLF physiology tape until treatment was completed, after which the recording was
erased from his mind. The sole exceptions to this rule
were senior physicians with teaching duties, which required the retention of one or two tapes, and the diagnosticians.

A diagnostician was one of the hospital elite, a
being whose mind was considered stable enough to
retain six, seven, and in a few cases, ten physiology
tapes simultaneously. To these data-crammed minds
were given projects such as original research in
xenological medicine and the treatment of new diseases in hitherto unknown life-forms.

But the tapes did not impart only physiological
data. Rather, the complete memory and personality
of the entity who had possessed that knowledge was
transferred as well. In effect, a diagnostician subjected
himself or itself voluntarily to the most drastic form of
schizophrenia. The entities apparently sharing a
diagnostician's mind could well be aggressive, unpleasant individuals—geniuses, whether medical or
otherwise, were rarely pleasant people—with all sorts
of peeves and phobias.

The original personality was never submerged completely, but depending on the case or research project
currently being worked on and the depth of concentration required for it, one could never be sure of a diagnostician's reaction to any request that was not of a
medical nature. Even then it was considered good
manners to find out who or what kind of personality
was in partial mental control of the entity concerned
before saying anything at all. As a class they were not
people one gave orders to, and even the hospital's
Chief Psychologist O'Mara had to treat them with a
certain degree of circumspection.

" . . . So I'm afraid you can't just tell them to go

away, Captain," Murchison went on, "and the seniors accompanying those diagnosticians will have sound medical reasons, as well as non-medical ones, for being here. You should also remember that for the past two weeks they have been checking us practically cell by cell, and they might become even more thorough if we were to suggest that they stop wasting time talking history to the scoutship crew and—"

"Not that," said the Captain hurriedly, and sighed. "But Thornnastor seems a friendly enough being, if a bit big and awkward, and it is our most frequent visitor. Could you suggest to it, ma'am, that if it came less often and without its medical retinue . . . ?"

Murchison shook her head firmly. "Thornnastor is Diagnostician-in-Charge in Pathology and as such is the hospital's senior diagnostician. It is also a source of news, a friend, and my head of department. Anyway, I enjoy Thorny's visits. You may think it odd that a Tralthan FGLI, an oversized, elephantine, six-legged, warm-blooded oxygen-breather with four manipulatory appendages and more eyes than seems decent should relish discussing a juicy piece of gossip from the SNLU section of the methane wards. You may even wonder how anything of a scandalous nature could occur between two intelligent crystalline entities living at minus one hundred and fifty degrees centigrade, or why their off-duty activities are of such interest to a warm-blooded oxygen-breather. But you must understand that Thorny's feeling for other e-ts, and even for us Earth-humans, is unique. It is, you see, one of our most stable and well-integrated multi-personalities . . ."

Fletcher held up both hands in a gesture of surrender. "As well as possessing the ability to instill a degree of personal loyalty in its staff, which is unusual, to say the least. All right, ma'am, you've convinced me. I am no longer ignorant about diagnosticians, and I can do nothing about their overrunning my ship."

"I'm afraid not, Captain," Murchison agreed sympathetically. "Only O'Mara could do something about that. But he is very fond of his diagnosticians and of saying that any being sane enough to be a diagnostician is mad . . . "

While Murchison and Fletcher had been speaking, the illumination in the dining compartment had undergone a subtle change, caused by the vision screen lighting up to show the craggy features of the Chief Psychologist.

"Why is it that every time I break in on a conversation I find people talking about me," O'Mara asked sourly. "But don't apologize or explain; you would strain my credulity. Conway, Fletcher, I have news for you. Doctor, you can discard that spacesuit, reconnect your cabin to the ship's air system, and resume eating and direct physical contact with your colleagues." He smiled faintly, but did not look at Murchison as he went on. "The ship has been cleared as free from infection, but frankly, this business has uncovered a serious weakness in patient reception procedures.

"Up until now," he continued, "we have assumed, and rightly, that new patients or casualties pose no threat because e-t pathogens cannot affect entities of another species. And because any being traveling in space, even on an interplanetary hop, has to undergo strict health checks, we tended to be a bit lax regarding same-species infections. That is why we are being very cautious and are allowing only the *Tenelphi* crew off the ship while the rest of you must stay aboard the *Rhabwar* for another five days. They caught the disease first, then the ambulance ship crew did; if you don't come down with symptoms during the next five days, then your ship and everyone on it is clear. However, to keep you and everyone else from feeling bored with inaction we have a job for you. Captain Fletcher, you and your officers are returned to active duty. How soon can you be ready to leave?"

Fletcher tried hard not to show his eagerness as he replied: "We have been unofficially on active duty for the past week and the ship is ready, Major. Provided we can have immediate action in the matter of topping up stores and medical consumables and there are no oversized e-ts getting underfoot—"

"That I can promise," said O'Mara.

"—we can take off within two hours," Fletcher ended.

"Very well," replied the Chief Psychologist briskly. "You will be answering a distress beacon detected in Sector Five, well out on the rim. The radiation signature of the beacon indicates that it is not one of ours. There is no Federation traffic out there anyway, and the star density is so low that we didn't waste time trying to chart the area ourselves. But if there *is* a star-traveling race out there, they might let us copy their charts when we show them ours. Especially if you bail some of their friends out of trouble. Or perhaps I should not remind highly altruistic medical types like yourselves of the mutual profit aspect of this situation. Communications Center will let you have the co-ordinates of the beacon presently. The probability of this distress signal originating from a ship of a hitherto undiscovered species is close to being a certainty.

"And Conway," O'Mara ended dryly, "this time try to bring back a few ordinary, or even extraordinary, casualties, and not a potential epidemic ..."

They wasted no time moving out to Jump distance because Fletcher was now fully confident of the capabilities of his ship. He did complain a little, although it seemed to Conway to be more in the nature of an apology, about the tuition during the first mission and this one. Theoretically, his officers and the medical team were supposed to become less specialized in their functions.

According to the ambulance-ship project directive, Conway was supposed to teach his officers the rudiments of e-t physiology, their physical structures, musculatures, circulatory systems and so on—enough of the subject, at least, for them not to kill some hapless casualty through good intentions. Meanwhile, Fletcher was supposed to reciprocate by lecturing the medical team on his particular specialty, e-t ship design and comparative technology, so that they would not make elementary errors regarding the vessel surrounding their patient.

Fletcher agreed with Conway that there would be no time to set up the lecture program on this mission, but that they would keep it in mind for the future. The result was that Conway spent most of the time in hyperspace with Naydrad, Prilicla and Murchison on the Casualty Deck, wondering whether they were properly prepared to receive an unknown number of casualties of an unknown physiological type. But he was in Control, at Fletcher's invitation, just before they were due to emerge.

A few seconds after the *Rhabwar* emerged into normal space, Lieutenant Dodds announced, "Wreckage ahead, sir."

"I don't believe . . . !" Fletcher began incredulously. "The accuracy of your astrogation is much too good, Dodds, to be due to anything but sheer luck."

"Oh, I don't know, sir," Dodds replied, grinning. "Distance is twelve miles. I'm locking on the scope now. You know, sir, this could be the fastest rescue ever recorded."

The Captain did not reply. He was looking pleased and excited and a little bit wary of so much good luck. On the screen the wreckage showed as a flickering gray blur spinning rapidly in the blackness. Out here on the Rim the stellar density was low, and most of the available light came from the long, faintly shining fog bank, which was the parent galaxy. Suddenly the image became brighter but even more blurred as Dodds switched to the infrared receptors and they saw the wreckage by its own heat radiation.

"Sensors?" the Captain asked.

"Non-organic material only, sir," Haslam reported. "No atmosphere present. Relative to the ambient temperature, it is very warm, suggesting that whatever happened occurred recently and probably as a result of an explosion."

Before the Captain could reply, Dodds said, "More wreckage, sir. A larger piece. Distance fifty-two miles. Spinning rapidly."

"Give me the numbers for closing with the larger

piece," Fletcher ordered. "Power Room, I want maximum thrust available in five minutes."

"Three more pieces," said Dodds. "Large, distance one hundred plus miles, widely divergent bearings, sir."

"Show me a distribution diagram," said the Captain, responding quickly. "Compute courses and velocities of all the pieces of wreckage, with a view to tracing the original point of the explosion. Haslam, can you tell me anything?"

"Same temparatures and material as the other pieces, sir," Haslam reported. "But they are at the limit of sensor range, and I could not say with certainty that it is composed entirely of metal. None of the pieces encloses an atmosphere, even residual."

"So if organic material is present," said Fletcher grimly, "it is no longer alive."

"More wreckage, sir," said Dodds.

This is not going to be a fast rescue, thought Conway. *It might not even be a rescue at all.*

Fletcher must have been reading Conway's mind, because he pointed at the big repeater screen. "Don't give up hope, Doctor. The first indications are that a ship has suffered a catastrophic explosion, and the distress beacon was released automatically as a result of the malfunction and not by one of the survivors, if any. But look at that display . . . "

The picture on the screen did not mean very much to Conway. He knew that the winking blue spot was the *Rhabwar* and that the white traces that were appearing every few seconds were wreckage detected by the ship's expanding radar and sensory spheres. The fine yellow lines that converged at the center of the screen were the computed paths taken by the wreckage from the point of the explosion, and what should have been a simple picture was confused by groups of symbols and numbers that flickered, changed or burned steadily beside every trace.

" . . . The distribution of the wreckage seems a bit lopsided for an explosion," Fletcher went on, "and although the scale is too small for it to be apparent on the screen, it appears to have originated from a short, flat arc rather than a point. Then, there is the virtually uniform rate of spin on the pieces of wreckage, and their relatively small number and large size. When a ship is torn apart by an explosion, usually caused by a power-reactor malfunction, debris size is small and the rate of spin negligible. Also, the temperature of this wreckage is too low for it to have originated in a reactor explosion, which we now know would have to have occurred less than seven hours ago.

"The probability is," the Captain ended, "that it was a hyperdrive generator malfunction, Doctor, and not an explosion."

Conway tried to control his irritation at the other's lecturing and faintly condescending tone, realizing that the Captain could not help his academic background. Conway knew that if one of a matched set of hyperdrive generators was to fail, the other was supposed to cut out automatically; the vessel concerned would emerge suddenly into normal space somewhere between the stars, and sit there, unable to make it home on impulse drive, until either it repaired the sick generator or help arrived. But there had been instances when the safety cutoff on the good generator had failed or had been a split second late in functioning, which meant that a part of the ship had been proceeding at hyperspeed while the rest had been slowed instantenously to sublight velocity. The effect on the vessel concerned was, at best, only slightly less catastrophic than a reactor explosion—but at least there would be no heat fusion, radiation and the other complications of a reactor blowup to worry about. The chance of finding survivors was very slightly increased.

"I understand," said Conway. He flipped the intercom switch on his console and said, "Casualty Deck, Conway here. You may stand down. Nothing will be happening for at least two hours."

"That is a pretty accurate estimate," Fletcher said dryly. "Since when have you become an astrogator, Doctor? Never mind. Dodds, compute a course linking the three largest pieces of wreckage, and put the figures on the Power Room repeater. Chen, we will apply maximum thrust in ten minutes. To save time I

plan to make a close pass of the likeliest prospects and
decelerate only if Haslam's sensors or Doctor Prilicla's
empathy say it is worth doing so. Haslam, stay on the
sensors and pick out a few more possibilities for us to
look at once we've checked the first three. And continue searching the radio frequencies in case a survivor is trying to attract our attention in that fashion,
and keep an eye on your scope in case it is trying to
flash a light at us."

As Conway was leaving the Control Deck to rejoin
his medical team aft, Haslam said in a quiet, respectful voice, "I've only got two eyes, sir, and they don't
swivel independently . . . "

One hour and fifty-two minutes later they passed
heart-stoppingly close to the first piece of wreckage.
The sensors had already reported negatively on it—
no organic material present other than structural
plastic trimming panels and furniture, no pockets of
atmosphere that might have contained a living entity.
When they tried to put a tractor beam on it to check
its spin, the whole mass began to fly apart and they
had to take violent evasive action.

They caught up with the next piece in less than an
hour. They had to decelerate and return to it, because
the sensors reported small pockets of atmosphere inside the wreckage and organic material of a non-
structural but not necessarily still-living kind. This
time they did not risk trying to check its spin in case
the loose mass of wreckage fell apart and the poten-
tially life-giving pockets of air were lost to space. Instead, they set the sensor and vision recorders going
during their slow, careful and extremely close approach. The close approach was for Prilicla's benefit,
but the empath reported apologetically that none of
the organic material was alive.

They had three hours to study the recordings before
reaching the third piece of wreckage, which was the
largest and most promising to be detected. In the
process they learned quite a lot about the design
philosophy of the alien ship-builders from the way the
structural members and bulkheads had been twisted
apart by the accident. The dimensions of the cor-

ridors and compartments gave an indication of the size of the life-forms that had crewed the ship. They had glimpses of things that looked like thick pieces of many-colored fur trapped and partially hidden in the wreckage. It might have been floor covering or bedding, except that a few of the pieces were restrained by webbing and many of them showed patches of reddish brown, which looked very much like dried blood.

"Judging by the color of those stains," Murchison observed as they studied one of the stills on the Casualty Deck repeater, "the chances are pretty good that they are warm-blooded oxygen-breathers. But do you think anyone could survive a disaster like that?"

Conway shook his head but tried to sound optimistic. "The staining on the fur does not appear to be associated with lacerations or punctured wounds of the kind suffered through violent deceleration or collision when the restraining body harness becomes deeply embedded in the body it was meant to protect. From these pictures it is impossible to tell which end of the body is which, but the staining seems to be located in the same areas of all the bodies. This suggests explosive decompression and the exiting of body fluid through natural openings, rather than massive external injury due to a sudden deceleration or collision. None of these people was wearing spacesuits, but if any of them was fast enough or lucky enough to be wearing suits, they should have been able to survive."

Before Murchison could reply the picture changed abruptly to show another mass of wreckage, and the excited voice of the Captain sounded from the wall speaker. "This looks like the best bet so far, Doctor. No spin to speak of, so we can board easily, if necessary. The fog you see is not all escaped air; some of it is boil-off from the vessel's water and hydraulic systems. If air is escaping, then there must be quite a lot of it still left on board. There is also what seems to be an emergency power circuit in use, weak and probably used for standby lighting. We may want to board this one. Is everyone ready?"

"Ready, friend Fletcher," said the empath.

"Of course," said Naydrad.

"We'll be at the Casualty lock in ten minutes," said Conway.

"Lieutenant Dodds and myself will accompany you," said the Captain, "in case structural or engineering problems are encountered. Ten minutes, Doctor."

There was not a lot of room to spare in the Casualty airlock with the Captain, Dodds, Naydrad and its already inflated pressure litter, Prilicla and Conway all clinging to its deck and walls with foot and wrist magnets while they watched the approach of the wreckage. It looked like a great rectangular metal thicket shrouded in fog and surrounded by smaller clumps of metal, some of which were spinning rapidly and some of which drifted motionless. When Conway asked why this should be, the Captain turned silent in the manner of a person who has asked himself the same question and was unable to answer. They waited while the ambulance ship edged closer, passing between two of the wreckage's madly spinning satellites, and their suit spotlights as well as those of the ship reflected off the twisted metal plating and projecting structural members. They went on waiting until the little Cinrusskin began trembling inside its spacesuit.

"Someone," Prilicla finally managed to utter, "is alive in there."

Of necessity, it was a hurried but very careful search, because the emotional radiation of the survivor was weak and characteristic of a mind that was becoming more deeply unconscious by the minute. With Prilicla indicating if not leading the way, the Captain and Dodds cleared a path through obstructions with their cutters or pushed away free-floating debris and tangled cable looms with their insulated gauntlets—there was, after all, a live power circuit in use. Conway followed closely behind, pulling himself along in a kind of weightless crawl through corridors and compartments whose ceilings were only four feet high.

Twice his spotlight picked out the bodies of crew-

members, which he freed and pushed gently back the
way they had come so that the waiting Naydrad could
load them into the unpressurized section of the litter.
Should the survivor need urgent surgical attention,
Conway would feel much better if Murchison had a
few cadavers to take apart so that she could tell him
how the living one should be put together again.

He still had no clear idea of what they looked like,
because the bodies had been encased in spacesuits.
But the suits and underlying tissue had been ruptured
by violent contact with metallic debris, and if the re-
sulting wounds had not killed the beings, the decompression had. Judging by the shape of the spacesuits,
the beings were flattened cylinders about six feet long
with four sets of manipulatory appendages behind a
conical section that was probably the head, and another four locomotor appendages. There was a
marked thickening at what was presumably the rear
section of the suit. Apart from the smaller size and
number of appendages, the beings physically resembled the Kelgian race, to which Naydrad belonged.

Conway could hear the Captain muttering to himself about the spacesuited aliens as they stopped at the
entrance to a compartment that retained pressure.
Prilicla felt carefully with its empathic faculty for the
presence of life, in vain. The survivor was located
somewhere beyond the compartment, the empath
said. Before the Captain and Dodds burned away the
door, Conway drilled through to obtain an atmosphere
sample for Murchison so that she could prepare suitable life-support for the survivor.

Inside the compartment there was light—a warm,
orange light, which would give important information
about the planet of origin and the visual equipment of
this species. But right then it illuminated only a sham-
bles of drifting furniture, twisted wall plating, tangles
of plumbing, and aliens, some of whom were spacesuited and all of whom were dead.

The thickened section at the rear of their spacesuits, Conway saw suddenly, was there to accommodate a large, furry tail.

"This is *collision* damage, dammit!" Fletcher burst out. "Losing a hypergenerator wouldn't have done all *this!*"

Conway cleared his throat. "Captain, Lieutenant Dodds, I know we haven't time to gather material for a major research project, but if you see anything in the way of photographs, paintings, illustrations, anything that would give me information about the alien's physiology and environment, take it along, please." He picked out another alien cadaver that was not too badly damaged, noting the pointed, fox-like head and the thick, broad-striped coat that made it look like a furry, short-legged zebra with an enormous tail. "Naydrad," he called, "here's another one for you."

"Yes, that must be it," the Captain said, half to himself. To Conway he added, "Doctor, these people were doubly unlucky, and the survivor doubly lucky . . . "

According to Fletcher, the hypergenerator failure had pulled the ship apart and sent the pieces spinning away. But in this particular place a number of the crew had survived and had managed to climb into their suits. They might even have had some warning of the approach of the second disaster—the overtaking of their section by another and equally massive piece of wreckage. When the collision occurred, the forward end of the first piece must have been swinging down while the afterpart of the second was swinging upwards. The kinetic energy of both sections had been cancelled out, bringing them both to rest and practically fusing them together. That, in the Captain's opinion, was the only explanation for the type of injuries and damage that had occurred here, and for the fact that this was the only section of the alien ship that was not spinning.

"I think you're right, Captain," said Conway, fishing out of the drifting mass of debris a flat piece of plastic with what looked like a landscape on one side of it. "But surely all this is academic now."

"Of course it is," Fletcher replied. "But I dislike unanswered questions. Doctor Prilicla, where now?"

The little empath pointed diagonally upwards at

the compartment's ceiling. "Fifteen to twenty meters in that direction, friend Fletcher, but I must admit to some feelings of confusion. The survivor seems to be moving slowly since we entered this compartment."

Fletcher sighed noisily. "A spacesuited and still mobile survivor," he said in relieved tones. "That will make the rescue very much easier." He looked at Dodds, and together they began cutting through the roof plating.

"Not necessarily," said Conway. "We could have a rescue and a first-contact situation both at the same time. I much prefer new and injured e-ts to be unconscious so that first contact can be made following curative treatment and we can exercise more control over the—"

"Doctor," the Captain broke in, "surely a star-traveling species, with the technical and philosophical background which that capability implies, would be expecting to meet what it would consider extraterrestrials. Even if they did not have the expectation, they surely would realize that there was a strong possibility of it happening."

"Granted," said Conway, "but an e-t who is injured and only partly conscious might react instinctively, illogically, to the sight of an alien being who might physically resemble a natural enemy or a predator on its home planet. And the treatment of a conscious extraterrestrial, a stranger who has no prior knowledge of the beings carrying out the treatment, might be mistaken for something else—torture, perhaps, or medical experimentation. All too often a doctor has to be cruel to be kind.'"

At that moment a large, circular section of the ceiling came free, its edges still bright red with the heat of the cutting torches, and was pushed away by Dodds and the Captain. As it followed them through the gap, Prilicla said, "I'm sorry if I confused you, friends. The survivor is moving slowly, but it is too deeply unconscious to move itself."

Their spotlights played over a compartment that was open to space in several places, filled with drifting masses of debris, containers of various sizes, a shoal

of bright objects that were probably sealed food pack-
ages, shelving and the bodies of three unsuited aliens,
which were torn and swollen by the twin effects of
massive external injuries and explosive decompression. The lights of the *Rhabwar* shone brightly through
an open tangle of metal, illuminating the areas where
their spotlights did not reach.

"It's here?" asked Fletcher in disbelief.

"It *is* here," said Prilicla.

The empath was indicating a large metal cabinet,
drifting slowly past on the outer fringes of the wreckage. The container was deeply scratched and fur-
rowed by violent contact with other metal, and there
was one dent in particular that was at least six inches
deep. There was a slight haze around the object, indicating that the air trapped inside was escaping
slowly.

"Naydrad!" Conway called urgently. "Forget your
pressure litter. The survivor has provided one of its
own, but it is depressurizing. We'll push it outside
where you can see it, then you can pull it on board
with a tractor. As fast as you can, Naydrad."

"Doctor," the Captain asked as they were maneuvering the cabinet through a gap in the wreckage, "do
we spend time here looking for information on this
species, or do we go on looking for other survivors?"

"We go looking, Captain," responded Conway
without hesitation. "With luck, the survivor will tell us
all we want to know about its species during convalescence . . . "

When the cabinet had been transferred to the Casualty Deck, the Captain examined its door actuator.
He said that the operating mechanism was straight-
forward and that the strength of the door and its
surrounding structure had kept that particular face of
the cabinet from being deformed during the collision.

"He means the door will open," Dodds translated
dryly.

Fletcher glared at the lieutenant. "The question is,
Should we open it without taking precautions—more
precautions than you are taking now, Doctor?"

Conway finished drilling, and he withdrew an air

sample from the cabinet interior before replying. As
he handed the sample to Murchison for analysis, he
said, "Captain, the box does *not* contain an Earth-
human DBDG with influenza. We *will* find an e-t of
a hitherto unknown species in urgent need of medical
attention, and as I have already explained, we are in
no danger from extraterrestrial pathogens."

"I keep worrying about the exception that might
prove the rule, Doctor," the Captain replied doggedly.
But he unsealed his visor to show everyone that he
was not too badly worried.

"Doctor Prilicla, please," came Haslam's voice
from Control. "Minus ten minutes."

The little empath hovered briefly over the cabinet,
assured them that there was no marked change in the
survivor's emotional radiation—it was still deeply
unconscious, but far from being terminal—and hurried to the airlock so that when the astrogator made a
close approach to the next mass of wreckage Prilicla
would be able to ascertain whether or not anything
had survived in it. As the Cinrusskin left, Murchison
straightened up from the analyzer display.

"If we assume that the first sample was taken from
a compartment at normal atmospheric composition
and pressure," she said, "then, apart from a few in-
nocuous trace elements that our ship atmosphere does
not contain, we would be quite happy breathing the
same air as they do. But the sample from the cabinet
is at half normal pressure and is high in carbon dioxide and water vapor. In short, the air inside that
cabinet is dangerously thin and stale, and the sooner
we get that beastie out of there the better."

"Right," said Conway. He removed the sampling
drill without sealing the hole it had made, and as the
Casualty Deck's air whistled into the cabinet, he said,
"Open her up, Captain."

The cabinet was lying on its back with the door
fastening, a rectangular metal plate with three conical
indentations on it, facing upwards. Fletcher pulled off
one of his gauntlets, pressed three fingers hard into the
impressions and slid the plate aside. They heard a

loud click, then he lifted the door open. Inside was a confused, bloody mess.

It took Conway several minutes to realize what had happened and to withdraw the bloodstained clothing or bedding from around the survivor. The cabinet had once contained upwards of twenty shelves, which had been pulled out hastily and the metal shelf supports padded with bedding or clothing to protect the occupant. But the collision had been a violent one, and there had been no time to attach the padding properly to the supports. As a result, both the padding and the survivor had been tumbled about the interior of the cabinet. The hapless e-t was jammed tightly into one end of the box, still bleeding sluggishly from a great many lacerations made by the shelf supports, and the colored bands of fur could barely be seen through tufted and matted patches of dried blood.

Very gently Murchison and Naydrad helped Conway lift out the survivor and lay it on the examination table. One of the gashes in its side began to bleed more freely, but as yet they did not know enough about the being to risk using one of their coagulants. Conway began going over its body with his scanner. "There must not have been any spacesuits in that compartment. But they must have had a few minutes' warning, enough for this one to clear and pad the cabinet and get inside, leaving the other three we saw to—"

"No, Doctor," said the Captain. He indicated the airtight cabinet. "It cannot be closed or opened from inside. The four of them must have decided which one was to survive, and they did their best for it, very quickly and, I should say, with minimum argument. As a species they seem to be very . . . civilized."

"I see," said Conway without looking up.

He did not know if there was any minor displacement of the survivor's internal organs, but his scanner indicated that none of the major ones were damaged or radically out of position. The spine also appeared to be undamaged, as did the elongated rib cage. On the back just above the root of the thick, furry tail was a bright pink area, which Conway thought at first was a patch where the fur was missing. But closer examination showed that it was a natural feature, and there were large flakes of what appeared to be some kind of pigment adhering to it. The being's head, which was tucked against its underside and partially covered by the tail, was conical, rodent-like and thickly furred. The skull itself appeared intact, but there was evidence of subcutaneous bleeding in several areas, which in a being without facial fur would have shown as massive bruising. There was some bleeding from the mouth, but Conway could not be sure whether it was due to an external blow or was the effect of lung damage caused by decompression.

"Help me straighten the poor thing out," he said to Naydrad. "It looks as if it tried to roll itself into a ball. Probably an instinctive defense posture it adopts when threatened by natural enemies."

"That is one of the things that puzzles me about this patient," said Murchison, looking up from her examination of one of the cadavers. "These creatures do not possess natural weapons of offense or defense as far as I can tell, or any signs of having had any in the past. Considering the fact that it is a planet's dominant life-form that develops intelligence, I don't see how these creatures came to dominate. Even their limbs are not built for speed, so they could not run from danger. The set used for walking are too short and are padded, while the forward set are more slender, less well-muscled and end in four highly flexible digits that don't possess so much as a fingernail among them. There are the fur markings, of course, but it is rare that a life-form rises to the top of its evolutionary tree by camouflage alone, or by being nice and cuddly. This is strange."

"It sounds like it comes from a nice world," said Prilicla, who had returned briefly from its airlock duty, "for Cinrusskins."

Conway did not join in the conversation, because he was reexamining the patient's lungs. The slight oral bleeding had worried him, and now that the survivor was properly presented for examination there was unmistakable evidence of decompression damage in the lungs. But moving the patient into the supine position had caused some of the deeper lacerations to start bleeding again. He could do very little about the lung damage with the facilities available on the ambulance ship, but considering the weakened state of the patient, the bleeding would have to be stopped quickly.

"Do you know enough about the composition of this beastie's blood at present," Conway asked Murchison, "to suggest a safe coagulant and anesthetic?"

"Coagulant, yes. Anesthetic, doubtful," Murchison replied. "I'd prefer to wait until we get back to the hospital for that. Thornnastor would be able to suggest, or synthesize, a completely safe one. Is it an emergency?"

Before Conway could reply, Prilicla chimed in: "An anesthetic is unnecessary, friend Conway. The patient is deeply unconscious and will remain so. It is in a slowly deteriorating condition, probably caused by impaired oxygen absorption in the damaged lungs, and the loss of blood would be a contributing factor. Those cabinet-shelf supports were like blunt knives."

"I agree," said Conway. "And if you're trying to suggest that the patient should be hospitalized as soon as possible, I agree with that too. But this one is in no immediate danger, and I would like to be sure that there are no other survivors before we leave. However, if you continue to monitor its emotional radiation and report any sudden change in—"

"More wreckage coming up," Haslam's voice broke in from the wall speaker. "Doctor Prilicla to the airlock, please."

"Yes, friend Conway," said the empath as it scuttled rapidly across the ceiling on its way to the lock.

Before he could begin treating the survivor's surface injuries, he had to quell a minor revolt by Naydrad, who, in common with all of its beautiful silver-furred race, had an intense aversion towards any surgical procedure that would damage or disfigure a being's most treasured possession, its fur. To a Kelgian the removal of a strip or patch of fur, which in their species represented a means of communication equal to the spoken word, was a personal tragedy that all too often resulted in permanent psychological damage. A Kelgian's fur did not grow again, and one whose pelt was damaged could rarely find a mate willing to accept a Kelgian who was unable to display fully its feelings. Murchison had to assure the charge nurse that the survivor's fur was not mobile and emotion-expressive and that it would undoubtedly grow again before Naydrad was content. It did not, of course, refuse to assist Conway during the minor surgery; it simply argued, both vocally and with its rippling and twitching fur, while it was shaving and cleaning the operative field.

Murchison broke in occasionally while they were suturing and applying coagulant to the wounds crisscrossing the patient's body, giving them odd items of information gleaned from her continuing examination and dissection of the cadavers.

The species had two sexes, male and female, and the reproductive system seemed relatively normal. Unlike the patient, however, whose fur appeared duller and to have less color variation, the cadavers of both sexes had applied a water-soluble dye that enhanced artificially the bands of color on their body fur, which otherwise would have been of the same intensity as those of the patient. Clearly the dyes were applied for cosmetic reasons. But why the patient, who was female, had not used dye on its fur was something unclear to Murchison.

One reason might be that the survivor was not yet fully mature and there was some cultural reason why a preadolescent of the species did not use or was forbidden to use cosmetics. Or it might be that the patient was mature and small, or of a race within the species that did not believe in painting its fur. An equally valid reason might be that the disaster had occurred before it had a chance to apply cosmetics. The only substance at all resembling cosmetic material had been the few pieces of flaking brownish pigment adhering to the patient's bare patch above its tail, and that material had been removed during pre-op procedure. The action of its friends, or possibly its family, in placing the survivor in an airtight cabinet just before the collision led Murchison to believe that it was a young and probably preadolescent female, rather than a small mature female.

The Federation had yet to encounter an intelligent species in which the adults would not sacrifice themselves to save their young.

While they were busying themselves with the one living and three dead aliens, Prilicla returned from the lock from time to time to report negatively on the search for other survivors—and similarly on the one they had rescued, whose condition, according to the empath's reading, was still deteriorating. Conway waited until Prilicla had been called to the airlock once again, not wanting to inconvenience the Cinrusskin with what could well be a flood of unpleasant emotional radiation; then he called Fletcher in Control.

"Captain, I have to make a decision and I need your advice," Conway said. "We have completed running repairs on our survivor, so far as the superficial injuries are concerned, but there is decompression damage to the lungs, which requires urgent hospitalization. As an interim measure, we have it on an enriched-oxygen-content air supply. Despite this, its condition is deteriorating, not rapidly but steadily. What, in your opinion, are the chances of picking up other survivors if we are to remain in this area for another four hours?"

"Virtually nil, Doctor," the Captain replied.

"I see." Conway had expected the answer to be much more complicated and hedged with probability computations and verbal qualifiers. He felt both relieved and worried.

"You must understand, Doctor," Fletcher went on, "that the first three pieces of wreckage investigated offered the greatest possibilities of finding survivors, and since then, the likelihood of finding one has diminished sharply, as have the sizes of the collections of debris with every piece we look at. Unless you believe in miracles, Doctor, we are wasting our time here."

"I see," said Conway.

"If it will help you reach a decision, Doctor," the Captain went on, "I can tell you that subspace radio conditions are very good out here, and we have already made two-way contact with the survey and Cultural Contact cruiser *Descartes,* which I am required to do when evidence of a new intelligent species is discovered. As a matter of urgency the *Descartes* will investigate this wreckage with a view to obtaining all available data on the new species, and by analyzing the velocities and directions of those species, will roughly establish the alien ship's point of departure and its destination. There are relatively few stars out here, so they should locate the home planet and star system fairly easily, because they are specialists at that job. Quite possibly, communications will be established with the aliens within a few weeks, perhaps sooner. As well, the *Descartes* carries two planetary landers, which in space double as close-range search and rescue vessels. They won't have Prilicla on board, naturally, but those ships could cover the remaining wreckage much faster than we could, Doctor."

"When will the *Descartes* arrive?" Conway asked.

"Allowing for multiple Jump effects on the astrogation," said Fletcher, "four to five hours."

Conway made no attempt to hide his relief. "Right. If there are no survivors on the next piece of wreckage, let's head for home at once, Captain." He paused for a moment, looking at the survivor and the bodies of its friends who had not made it, then at Murchison. "If they find the home world and make contact quickly, will you ask the *Descartes* to request medical assistance for our friend here? Ask for a volunteer native medic to travel to Sector General to assist or, if necessary, to take charge of the treatment. In cases involving completely new life-forms we can't afford to be proud . . . "

He was also thinking that the native medic might, when it felt more at ease with the multiplicity of life-forms inhabiting the hospital, be agreeable to providing an Educator tape on its people so that the hospital staff would know exactly what they were doing if, on

some future occasion, another member of its species
became a patient.

"Identify yourself, please. Visitor, staff or patient,
and species?" came a toneless translated voice from
Reception a few minutes after they had emerged into
normal space. The hospital was still little more than
a large blurred star against a background of smaller,
brighter ones. "If you are unsure of, or are unable to
give, an accurate physiological classification because
of physical injury, mental confusion or ignorance of
the relevant data, please make vision contact."

Conway looked at Captain Fletcher, who drew
down the corners of his mouth and raised one eyebrow
in a piece of non-verbal communication which said
that the person who understood the medical jargon
was best fitted to answer the questions.

"Ambulance ship *Rhabwar,* Senior Physician Conway speaking," he responded briskly. "Staff and one
patient, all warm-blooded oxygen-breathing. Crew classifications are Earth-human DBDG, Cinrusskin GLNO
and Kelgian DBLF. The patient is a DBPK, origin
unknown. It has sustained injuries which will require
urgent—"

"You are expected, *Rhabwar,* and I have you flagged
as priority traffic," the voice from Reception broke in.
"Please use approach pattern Red Two and follow the
red-yellow-red beacons to Lock Five—"

"But Lock Five is a—"

"—which is, as you know, Doctor, the principal entry port to the levels of the water-breathing AUGLs,"
Reception continued. "However, the accommodation
being reserved for your casualty is close to Five; and
Three, which you would normally use, is tied up with
twenty-plus Hudlar casualties. There has been some
kind of structural accident with radiation side effects
during assembly of a Melfan orbiting factory, but I am
aware only of the clinical details at present.

"Thornnastor did not know what, if anything, you
were bringing in," Reception added, "but it thought it
better not to subject the casualty even to residual radiation. Your ETA, Doctor?"

Conway looked at Fetcher, who said, "Two hours, sixteen minutes."

That would be ample time for their DBPK casualty to be transferred into a pressure litter capable of maintaining the integrity of the patient's life-support system against hard vacuum, water and a wide variety of lethal atmospheres, and for the *Rhabwar*'s medical team to don lightweight suits, which would enable them to accompany it. The intervening time could also be used to transmit and to consult with Diagnostician-in-Charge Thornnastor regarding their preliminary findings on the DBPK survivor and the results of Murchison's examination of the cadavers. Thornnastor would probably request the early transfer of those cadavers so as to make a thorough investigation that would give a complete picture of the DBPK life-form's metabolism. Conway relayed the Captain's estimate and asked who would be meeting the *Rhabwar* medics at Lock Five.

The voice from Reception made a number of short, untranslatable noises, possibly the e-t equivalent of a stammer, then went on, "I'm sorry, Doctor. My instructions are that *Rhabwar* personnel are still technically in quarantine and may not enter the hospital. But you may accompany the casualty, provided you do not unseal. The assistance of your team will not be required, Doctor, but the proceedings will be broadcast on the teaching channels so that you will be able to observe and, if necessary, advise."

"Thank you," said Conway. The sarcasm was lost, naturally, in the translation.

"You're welcome, Doctor," said Reception. "And now can I have your communications officer. Diagnostician Thornnastor has requested a direct link with Pathologist Murchison and yourself for purposes of consultation and preliminary diagnosis . . ."

A little more than two hours later, Thornnastor knew all that it was possible to know about the casualty at a distance, and the patient in its pressure litter was being transferred very gently from the *Rhabwar*'s boarding tube into the cavernous entry port that was Lock Five. Prilicla was also allowed to accompany the

patient to monitor its emotional radiation. Reluctantly,
the hospital authorities had agreed that the little Cinrusskin was unlikely to carry with it the virus that had
affected the *Rhabwar*'s crew, and besides, it was the
only medically qualified empath currently on the hospital's staff.

The reception and transfer team—Earth-humans in
lightweight suits with the helmets, belts and boots
painted bright fluorescent blue—quickly moved the
pressure litter to Lock Five's inner seal. The outer seal
closed ponderously and water poured in, bubbling and
steaming coldly as it entered the recently airless chamber. By the time the turbulence had cleared and
Conway was able to see, the team was already man-
handling the litter into the tepid green depths of the
ward devoted to the treatment of the water-breathing
inhabitants of Chalderescol.

Conway was glad that their casualty was unconscious, because the Chalders, whose wide variety of
ailments rarely left them immobile, swam ponderously
around the litter, displaying the curiosity of all hospital patients towards anything that promised to break
the monotony of ward routine.

The ward resembled a vast undersea cavern, taste-
fully decorated, to Chalder eyes, with a variety of artificial native plant life, some of which was obviously
carnivorous. This was not the normal environment of
the natives of Chalderescol, who were highly advanced
both culturally and technically, but the type of surroundings sought by healthy young Chalders going on
vacation. According to Chief Psychologist O'Mara,
who was rarely wrong in these matters, the primitive
environment was a significant aid to recovery. But
even to an Earth-human DBDG like Conway, who
knew exactly what was going on, it was a spooky
place.

A completely new life-form whose language had yet
to be programed into the hospital's translation computer would not know what to think—especially if it was
confronted suddenly with one of the AUGL patients.

An adult native of Chalderescol resembled a forty-
foot-long crocodile, armor-plated from the rather over-

large mouth to the tail, and with a belt of ribbon
tentacles encircling its middle. Even with Prilicla present to radiate reassurance, it was much better for the
patient's peace of mind that it did not see the Chalder
AUGLs, who swam to within a few meters of the litter
to eye the newcomer and wish it well.

Prilicla drifted slightly ahead of the party, a vague
insect shape inside the silvery bubble of its suit, twitching occasionally to the bursts of emotional radiation in
the area. Conway knew from past experience that it
was not the casualty or the curious AUGL patients
who were responsible for this reaction, but the feelings
of the transfer team maneuvering the litter past the
sleeping frames, equipment and artificial flora of the
ward and the stretch of water-filled corridor beyond it.
The drying and cooling units in the team's issue
lightweight suits did not operate at peak efficiency in
the warm water of the AUGL level, and when
strenuous physical effort was called for in that environment, the tempers shortened in direct proportion
to the temperature rise.

The Observation Ward for the new patient had been
part of the Casualty Department's initial treatment
area for warm-blooded oxygen-breathers before that
facility had been moved to Level 33 and extended.
The intention had been to fit the original room as an
additional AUGL operating theater as soon as the engineering section could get around to it, but at the
present time it was still a large, square-sided bubble of
air and light inside the watery vastness of the Chalder
wards and service units. At the center of the room was
an examination table, adjustable to the body configu-
rations of a wide variety of physiological classifications and with provision for conversion to either an
operating table or a bed. Ranged along opposing walls
of the ward was the similarly non-specialized and complex equipment required for the life-support and intensive care of patients whose life processes were, at
times, a partly open book.

Although large, the room was overcrowded—mostly
with people who had no business being there and no
reason other than professional curiosity. Conway

could see one of the scaly, membranous Illensan
PVSJs, its loose protective suit transparent except for
the faint yellow fog of chlorine it contained, and there
was even a TLTU encased in a pressure sphere
mounted on caterpillar tracks, which was the only way
a being who breathed superheated steam at high pressure could associate professionally with patients and
colleagues with less exotic metabolisms. The remainder
were warm-blooded oxygen-breathers—Melfans, Kelgians, Nidians and one Hudlar—with one thing in
common besides their curiosity: the gold or gold-
edged ID badges of diagnosticians or senior physicians.

Rarely had Conway seen so much medical talent
concentrated in such a small area.

They all stayed well clear of the transfer team as
the patient was moved from the litter onto the examination table, supervised by Thornnastor itself. The litter was left unsealed and moved back to the ward
entrance so as to be out of the way; then everyone
began edging closer.

Murchison and Naydrad were watching on the
Rhabwar's screen, Conway knew, as Thornnastor began the preliminary examination, which was in all respects identical to the one carried out by Murchison
and Conway on the ambulance ship—a careful check
of the vital signs, even though at this stage nobody
could be quite sure what was or was not a normal
pulse, respiration or blood pressure reading for a
DBPK—followed by deep and detailed scanning and
gentle probing for physical injury or deformation.
While it worked, Thornnastor described in detail
everything it did, saw or deduced for the many medics
who were observing on the teaching channels. Occasionally it paused to ask questions of Murchison on
the ambulance ship or of Conway in the ward regarding the patient's condition immediately following its
rescue, and for any comments that might be helpful.

Thornnastor had reached its unrivaled eminence in
e-t pathology by asking questions and pondering the
answers, not by listening to itself pontificate.

Finally, Thornnastor's examination was complete.

It brought its massive body fully erect so that the osseous dome housing its brain was almost hidden by the curves of its massive triple shoulders. Its four extensible eyes regarded, simultaneously, the patient, the medics ranged around the examination table and the vision pickups through which the *Rhabwar* and the other non-present observers were viewing the proceedings. Then it spoke.

The most serious damage had been sustained by the patient's lungs, where decompression effects had ruptured tissue and caused widespread bleeding. Thornnastor proposed relieving this situation by withdrawing the unwanted fluid via a minor surgical intervention through the pleural cavity and into the trachea for the purpose of assisting the patient's breathing by positive pressure ventilation of the lungs with pure oxygen. There was a wide range of tissue-regenerative medication available for warm-blooded oxygen-breathers, but the tests that would be carried out on the DBPK cadavers to find one harmless to the DBPK species would be exhaustive and would require two days at least, by which time a safe anesthetic would also be available. Without immediate surgical intervention the patient would not live for more than a few hours. Neither of the proposed procedures was lengthy, the associated pain was minimal, and as Prilicla reported, the patient was too deeply unconscious to be aware of pain, so Thornnastor, assisted by a Melfan senior physician and a Kelgian theater nurse, would operate at once.

Considering the condition of the patient, Conway thought, it was the only sensible thing to do. He felt irked that it was not himself who was assisting Thornnastor, since he had had prior experience with the DBPK life-form. But then he realized, from listening to the respectful whispers coming from the other observers, that the Melfan senior assisting was Edanelt, one of the hospital's top e-t surgeons, the permanent possessor of four Educator tapes, and according to the grapevine, a being shortly to be elevated to diagnostician status. If a surgeon of Edanelt's eminence could be big enough to assist, then Conway should be able to watch without radiating too much envy.

It had never ceased to amaze Conway, despite the hundreds of operations he had seen Tralthans perform, that such a monstrous and physically ungainly species could produce the Federation's finest surgeons. The DBPK patient did not know how fortunate it was, because it was said in the hospital that no life-form, no matter how hopeless its case might be, was ever lost if it came under Thornnastor's personal care. Such a thing was unthinkable, Thornnastor was reputed to have said, because it was not in its contract . . .

"Consciousness is returning," Prilicla announced suddenly, barely ten minutes after the operation was complete. "It is returning very rapidly."

Thornnastor made a loud, untranslatable sound, which probably signified satisfaction and pleasure. "Such a rapid response to treatment promises a favorable prognosis and, I should think, an early recovery. But let us withdraw for a short distance. Even though a member of a star-traveling race is accustomed to seeing other life-forms, in its weakened state our patient might be worried by the close proximity of a group of such large and diverse beings as ourselves. You agree, Doctor Prilicla?"

But the little empath did not have a chance to reply, because the patient had opened its eyes and was struggling so violently against the body restraints that its tracheal air hose threatened to become detached.

Instinctively, Thornnastor reached over the patient to steady the air hose, and the DBPK became even more agitated. The emotion-sensitive Prilicla began trembling so violently that it was in danger of coming unstuck from the ceiling. Suddenly the patient stiffened and remained absolutely still for several minutes, but then it began to relax again as the Cinrusskin radiated sympathy and reassurance.

"Thank you, Doctor Prilicla," said Thornnastor. "When communication has been established, I shall apologize to this patient for nearly frightening it to death. In the meantime, try to let it know that we wish it well."

"Of course, friend Thornnastor. It is feeling concern now, rather than terror, and it seems to be deeply worried about something which . . ." Prilicla broke off and began to tremble violently.

What happened next was utterly impossible.

Thornnastor began to sway alarmingly on its six stubby legs, legs which normally gave the Tralthan species such a stable base that they frequently went to sleep standing up; then it toppled onto its side with a crash that overloaded the sound pickup on Conway's suit. A few yards away from the treatment table the Melfan Edanelt, who had been assisting Thornnastor, collapsed slowly to the floor, its six multijointed legs becoming progressively more limp until the underside of its exoskeletal body hit the floor with a loud click. The Kelgian theater nurse had also slipped to the floor, the silvery fur on its long, cylindrical body undulating and puckering as if being affected by a tiny whirlwind. A member of the transfer team standing beside Conway dropped loosely to his hands and knees, crawled for a short distance along the floor and then rolled onto his side. Too many e-ts began speaking at once, and Earth-humans trying to outshout them, for Conway's translator to produce anything intelligible.

"This can't be happening . . . " he began incredulously.

Murchison's voice sounded in his helmet phones, speaking on the ship frequency. "Three extraterrestrial life-forms and one Earth-human DBDG, with four radically different metabolisms and inherent species-immunity . . . it's quadruply impossible! As far as I see, no indications of the other unprotected life-forms being affected."

Even when observing the impossible, Murchison remained clinical.

" . . . But it *is* happening," Conway went on. He turned up the volume of his suit external speaker. "This is Senior Physician Conway. Instructions. All transfer team-members, seal your helmets. Team leader, sound the alarm for Contamination One. Everyone else, move away from the patient . . ." They were doing so already, Conway could see, with a degree of haste that verged on panic. "Beings already wearing protective suits stand clear, unprotected

oxygen-breathers go to the pressure litter and as many
as possible seal yourselves inside. Everyone else should
use the breathing masks and oxygen supplies for the
ward ventilators. We seem to be affected by some kind
of airborne infection—"

He broke off as the observation ward's main screen
flicked on to show the features of the irate Chief Psychologist. As O'Mara spoke Conway could hear in
the background the repeated long and two short blasts
on the emergency siren, which gave added urgency to
the words.

"Conway, why the blazes are you reporting lethal
contamination down there? Dammit, there can't be a
lethal contamination of air and water unless the place
is flooded and you're all drowning, and I see no evidence of that!"

"Wait," said Conway. He was kneeling by the fallen
transfer team-member, his hand inside the open visor,
feeling for a pulse at the temporal artery. He found it,
a fast, irregular beat that he did not like at all. Then
he sealed the man's visor quickly and went on speaking to the ward: "Remember to close any breathing
orifices not covered by your masks, nostrils, Melfan
gills, the Kelgian speaking mouth. And you, the protected Illensan doctor, will you check Thornnastor and
the Melfan Edanelt, quickly please. Prilicla, how is
the original patient?"

The chlorine-breather waddled rapidly towards the
fallen Thornnastor, its transparent suit rustling. "My
name is Gilvesh, Conway. But all DBDGs look the
same to me, so I suppose I should not feel insulted."

"Sorry, Gilvesh," said Conway. The chlorine-
breathing Illensans were generally held to be the most
visually repulsive species in the Federation as well as
the most vain regarding their own physical appearance. "A snap diagnosis, please. There isn't time for
anything else. What happened to it, and what are the
immediate physiological effects?"

"Friend Conway," said Prilicla, still trembling violently, "the DBPK patient is feeling much better. It is
radiating confusion and worry, but no fear and minimum physical discomfort. The condition of the other

four concerns me deeply, but their emotional radiation is too faint to identify because of the high level of emotion pervading the ward."

"I understand," said Conway, who knew that the little empath could never bring itself to criticize, however mildly, another being's emotional shortcomings. "Attention, everyone. Apart from the four people already affected there is no immediate sign of the condition, infection, whatever it is, spreading. I would say that anyone protected by the pressure litter envelope or breathing through a mask is safe for the time being. And calm yourselves, please. We need Prilicla to help with a quick diagnosis on your colleagues, and it can't work if the rest of you are emoting all over the place."

While Conway was still speaking, Prilicla detached itself from the ceiling and fluttered across on its iridescent wings to the heap of silvery fur that was the Kelgian theater nurse. It withdrew its scanner and began a physical examination concurrent with its efforts to detect, isolate and identify the creature's emotional radiation. It was no longer trembling.

"No response to physical stimuli," Gilvesh reported from its examination of Thornnastor. "Temperature normal, breathing labored, cardiac action weak and irregular, eyes still react to light, but . . . This is strange, Conway. Obviously the lungs have been seriously affected, but the mechanism is unclear, and the curtailed supply of oxygen is affecting the heart and brain. I can find no signs of lung-tissue damage of the kind associated with the inhalation of corrosive or highly toxic material, nor anything to suggest that its immune system has been triggered off. There is no muscular tension or resistance; the voluntary muscles appear to be completely relaxed."

Using his scanner without unsealing the lightweight suit, Conway had examined the team-member's upper respiratory tract, trachea, lungs and heart with exactly similar results. But before he could say anything, Prilicla joined in: "My patient displays similar symptoms, friend Conway," it said. "Shallow and irregular respiration, cardiac condition close to fibrillation, deepening unconsciousness and all the physical and emotional signs of asphyxiation. Shall I check Eda-nelt?"

"I'll do that," said Gilvesh quickly. "Prilicla, move clear lest I walk on you. Conway, in my opinion they require intensive-care therapy as soon as possible, and a breathing assist at once."

"I agree, friend Gilvesh," the empath said as it fluttered up to the ceiling again. "The condition of all four beings is extremely grave."

"Right," Conway agreed briskly. "Team Leader! Move your man, the DBLF and the ELNT clear and as far from the patient as possible, but close to an oxygen supply outlet. Doctor Gilvesh will supervise fitting the proper breathing masks, but keep your team-member sealed up, with his suit air supply at fifty percent oxygen. Regarding Thornnastor, you'll need the rest of your team to move—"

"Or an anti-gravity sled," the Team Leader broke in. "There's one on the next level."

"—it even a few yards," Conway went on. "Considering its worsening condition, it would be better to rig an extension to an oxygen line and assist Thornnastor's breathing where it is lying. And, Team Leader, do not leave the ward for a sled or anything else until we know exactly what it is that is loose in here. That goes for everyone . . . Excuse me."

O'Mara was refusing to remain silent any longer. "So there *is* something loose in there, Doctor?" said the Chief Psychologist harshly. "Something much worse, seemingly, than a simple case of atmospheric contamination from an adjacent ward? Have you finally discovered the exception that proves the rule, a bug that attacks across the species' lines?"

"I know Earth-human pathogens cannot affect e-ts, and vice versa," Conway said impatiently, turning to the ward screen to face O'Mara. "It is supposed to be impossible, but the impossible seems to be happening, and we need help to—"

"Friend Conway," Prilicla broke in, "Thornnastor's condition is deteriorating steadily. I detect feelings of constriction, strangulation."

"Doctor," the translated voice of Gilvesh joined in,

"the Kelgian's oxygen mask isn't doing much good. The DBLF double mouth and lack of muscle control is posing problems. Positive pressure ventilation of the lungs with direct access through the trachea is indicated to avoid a complete respiratory failure."

"Can you perform a Kelgian tracheotomy, Doctor Gilvesh?" Conway asked, turning away from the screen. He could not think of anything to do to help Thornnastor.

"Not without a tape," Gilvesh replied.

"No tape," said O'Mara firmly, "or anything else."

Conway swung round to face the image of the Chief Psychologist to protest, but he already knew what O'Mara was going to say.

"When you raised the lethal contamination alarm, Doctor," the Chief Psychologist went on grimly, "you acted instinctively, I should think, but correctly. By so doing you have probably saved the lives of thousands of beings inside the hospital. But a Contamination One alarm means that your area is isolated until the cause of the contamination has been traced and neutralized. In this case it is much more serious. There seems to be a bug loose that could decimate the hospital's warm-blooded oxygen-breathers. For that reason your ward has been sealed off. Power, light, communication and translation facilities are available, but you are no longer connected to the main air supply system or to the automatic food distribution network, nor will you receive medical consumables of any kind. Neither will any person, mechanism or specimen for analysis be allowed out of your area. In short, Doctor Gilvesh will not be allowed to come to me for a DBLF physiology tape, nor will any Kelgian, Melfan or Tralthan doctor be allowed to volunteer to go to the aid of the affected beings. Do you understand, Doctor?"

Conway nodded slowly.

O'Mara's craggy features showed a deep and uncharacteristic concern as he stared at Conway for several seconds. It was said that O'Mara's normally abrasive and sarcastic manner was reserved only for his friends, with whom he liked to relax and be his bad-tempered self, and that he was quiet and sympathetic only when he was professionally concerned about someone.

He has an awful lot of friends, Conway thought, *and right now I'm in trouble . . .*

"No doubt you would like to have the life-duration figures based on the residual and tanked air remaining in the ward, and the number and species of the present occupants," the Major continued. "I'll have them for you in a few minutes. And, Conway, try to come up with an answer . . . "

For several seconds Conway stared at the blank screen and told himself that there was nothing effective he could do about Thornnastor or Edanelt or the Kelgian nurse or the team-member—all of whom had suddenly switched their roles from medics to critically ill patients—without Educator tapes.

In the normal course of events Doctor Gilvesh would have taken a DBLF tape and performed a tracheotomy on the Kelgian as a matter of course, and the Illensan senior would probably have insisted on O'Mara giving it the Tralthan tape for Thornnastor and the ELNT one for Edanelt, provided the Chief Psychologist considered Gilvesh's mind stable enough to take three tapes for short-term use. But Gilvesh was not allowed to leave the ward even if its chlorine-breathing life depended on it, which it would very shortly.

Conway tried not to think about the diminishing supply of air remaining in the pressure litter, where five or six e-ts were rapidly using up the tanked oxygen; or of the other beings ranged along opposing walls who were connected to breathing masks intended for patients; or of the four-hour supply carried by the transfer team-members and himself, or of the air in the ward, which was infected and unusable, or even of the strictly limited amount of breathable chlorine carried by Gilvesh, or of the superheated atmosphere required by the TLTU. He had to think of the patients first, he told himself clinically, and try to keep them alive as long as possible. He would do this not because they were his friends and colleagues, but because they had been the first to be stricken and he had to chart the course of the infection as completely as possible so that the hospital medics of all grades and specialties would know exactly what they would have to fight.

But the fight would have to start here in the observation ward, and there were a few things Conway could do, or try to do.

"Gilvesh," he finally said, "go to the TLTU parked in the corner and the Hudlar on the mask beside it. I don't know if their translators can receive me at this distance. Ask them if they will move Thornnastor to the clear area of wall beside the lock entrance. If they can do it, warn them that Tralthans must not be rolled onto their backs under normal gravity conditions, since this causes organic displacement, which would increase its respiratory difficulties, and ask one of the transfer team to hold Thorny's mask in position while it is being moved.

"When it is at the wall," Conway went on, "position it with its legs pointing away from the wall and ask four team members to . . . "

While he talked Conway was thinking of all the Educator tapes he had had to digest during his career at Sector General and that, in a few cases, erasure had not been complete. None of the weird and wonderful personalities who had donated their brain recordings had remained, even in part, in his memory because that could have been psychologically dangerous. But there were odds and ends of data, pertaining chiefly to physiology and surgical procedures, which he had retained, because the Earth-human part of his mind had been particularly interested in them while the e-t personality had been in charge. The action he was considering taking with regard to the Kelgian theater nurse was dangerous—he had only the vaguest of memories regarding DBLF physiology in the respiratory tract area—and probably unprofessional. But first he had to do something for Thornnastor, even if it was little more than a first-aid measure.

The TLTU medic, whose race existed in an environment of edible minerals and superheated steam, had a protective suit that resembled a spherical pressure

boiler bristling with remote handling devices and
mounted on caterpillar treads. The vehicle had not
been designated to move unconscious Tralthans, but it
was quite capable of doing so.

The Hudlar doctor, classification FROB, was a
blocky, pear-shaped being whose home planet pulled
four Earth gravities and had a high-density atmosphere so rich in suspended animal and vegetable nu-
trients that it resembled thick soup. Although the
FROB life-form was warm-blooded and technically an
oxygen-breather, it could go for long periods without
air if its food supply, which it absorbed directly
through its thick but highly porous tegument, was adequate. The Hudlar's last meal had been sprayed on
less than two hours earlier, Conway estimated, judging by the flaking condition of its covering of nutrient
paint. It should be able to do without the oxygen mask
long enough to help Thornnastor.

". . . While they're moving Thornnastor," Conway
went on, speaking to the transfer team leader, "have
your men move the pressure litter as close as possible
to the Kelgian nurse. There is another Kelgian, a
diagnostician, inside the litter. Ask it if it would direct
me while I try to do the tracheotomy, and make sure
it has a good view of the operation through the envelope of the litter. I'll be there in a few minutes, as soon
as I check on Edanelt."

"Edanelt's condition is stable, friend Conway," reported Prilicla, who was keeping well clear of the
Hudlar and the hissing metal juggernaut of the TLTU,
who were moving Thornnastor. It made a feather-light
landing on the Melfan's carapace for a closer feel of
Edanelt's emotional radiation. "It is breathing with
difficulty but is in no immediate danger."

Of the three e-ts affected, it had been the farthest
away from the DBPK casualty—which should mean
something. Conway shook his head angrily. Too much
was happening at once. He was not being given a
chance to *think* . . .

"Friend Conway," called Prilicla, who had moved to
the DBPK casualty. "I detect feelings of increasing
discomfort not associated with its injuries—feelings of

constraint. It is also extremely worried, but not fearful, about something. The feeling is of intense guilt
and concern. Perhaps, in addition to the injuries sustained in its ship, there is a history of psychological
disturbance of the type common to certain preadoles-
cents . . . "

The mental state of the DBPK survivor was low on
Conway's order of priorities right then, and there was
no way he could conceal his impatience from Prilicla.

"May I ease its physical restraints, friend Conway?"
the empath ended quickly.

"Yes, just don't let it loose," Conway replied, then
felt stupid as soon as he finished speaking.

The small, furry, utterly inoffensive being did not
represent a physical threat—it was the pathogens it
carried that provided the danger, and they were already loose. But when Prilicla's fragile pipe-stem manipulators touched the buttons that reduced the tight-
ness of the restraining webbing holding the DBPK to
the examination table, it did not try to escape. Instead
it moved itself carefully until it lay like a sleeping
Earth cat, curled up with its head pushed underneath
its long and furry tail, looking like a mound of striped
fur except for the bare patch at the root of its tail
where the skin showed pinkish brown.

"It feels much more comfortable now, but is still
worried, friend Conway," the Cinrusskin reported.
Then it scuttled across the ceiling towards Thornnastor's position, trembling slightly because the unconscious diagnostician was experiencing strong emotions.

The TLTU had taped Thornnastor's rear legs together, then withdrawn to enable the Hudlar and four
team-members to do their work. With one man each
grasping a middle or forward leg, they strained to
pull them diagonally apart so as to expand the Tralthan's chest as much as possible. The Hudlar was saying, "Pull together. Harder. Hold it. Let go." When it
said "let go" the legs resumed their natural position
while simultaneously the Hudlar pressed on Thornnastor's massive rib-cage with its own not inconsider-
able weight to ensure that the lungs were deflated
before the process was repeated. Behind the visors of

the men tugging on Thornnastor's legs were faces deep
red and shining with perspiration, and some of the
things they were saying were not suitable for translation.

Every medic, orderly and maintenance man in Sector General was taught the rudiments of first aid as
it applied to members of the species that made up the
Galactic Federation—those, that is, whose environmental requirements were not so exotic that only another member of their race could aid them without
delay. The instructions for giving artificial respiration
to a Tralthan FGLI was to tie the rear legs together
and open and close the other four so as to suck air
into the FGLI's lungs. Thornnastor's mask was in
position, and it was being forced to breathe pure oxygen. Prilicla was available to report any change in its
condition.

But a Kelgian tracheotomy was most decidedly not
a first-aid measure. Except for a thin-walled, narrow
casing that housed the brain, the DBLF species had no
bone structure. The DBLF body was composed of an
outer cylinder of musculature, which, in addition to
being its primary means of locomotion, protected the
vital organs within it. The Kelgian life-form was dangerously susceptible to lethal injury, because the complex and highly vulnerable circulatory system that fed
those great bands of encircling muscle ran close under
the skin and was protected only by its thick fur. An
injury that most other species would consider superficial could cause a Kelgian to bleed to death in minutes. Conway's problem was that the Kelgian trachea
was deeply buried under the neck muscles and passed
within half an inch of the main artery and vein, which
carried the blood supply to and from the brain.

With an Earth-human surgeon operating to the verbal instructions of another Kelgian, and hampered by
the lack of a DBLF physiology tape and suit gauntlets,
the procedure promised to be both difficult and dangerous.

"I would prefer," the Kelgian diagnostician announced, its face pressed against the transparent wall

of the pressure litter, "to perform this operation my-self, Doctor."

Conway did not reply, because they both knew that if the diagnostician left the litter it would be open to the air of the ward and whatever form of infection it contained, as would the other occupants of the litter. Instead, he began removing a narrow patch of fur from the Kelgian nurse's neck while Gilvesh sterilized the area.

"Try not to shave off too much fur, Doctor," said the Kelgian diagnostician, who had given its name as Towan. "It will not grow again on an adult and the condition of its fur is of great psychological importance to a Kelgian, particularly in premating approaches to the opposite sex."

"I *know* that," said Conway.

As he worked Conway found that some of the memories he retained from the Kelgian physiology tapes were trustworthy, while many others were not. He was very glad of the voice from the litter, which kept him from going disastrously wrong. During the fifteen minutes it took to perform the operation, Towan fumed and fretted and poured out a constant stream of instruction, advice and warnings, which at times were indistinguishable from personal insults—the fellow-feeling among Kelgians was very strong. Then, finally, the operation and the abuse ended, and Gilvesh began preparing to connect the nurse to a ventilator while Conway walked across the ward to have a closer look at Thornnastor.

Suddenly the ward screen lit again, this time to show the faces of O'Mara and the Monitor Corps officer in charge of hospital supply and maintenance, Colonel Skempton. It was the Colonel who finally spoke.

"We have been calculating the time left to you using the air supply currently available in your ward, Doctor," he said quietly. "The people on breathing masks, provided the bug doesn't get to them through one of their other body orifices or they don't fall asleep and dislodge the masks, have about three days' supply of air. The reason for this is that the six ventilator systems in that ward each carry a ten-hour supply of oxygen as well as other gases which are of no interest to you in the current situation—nitrogen, CO_2 and the like. The transfer team-members each have a four-hour supply in their lightweight suits, providing they conserve their oxygen by resting as much as possible—"

The Colonel broke off, and Conway knew that he was staring at the four team-members who were helping the Hudlar give artificial respiration to Thornnastor; then he cleared his throat and went on: "The Kelgian, Nidian and three Earth-humans sheltering inside the litter have less than an hour's supply remaining. However, it is possible for the team-members to recharge the litter and their own suits with air from the ventilator supply as this becomes necessary. If this is done and everyone rests as much as possible, those of you who do not succumb to the bug should still be alive in, say, thirty hours, which gives us time to—"

"What about Gilvesh and the TLTU?" said Conway sharply.

"Recharging the TLTU's life-support system is a specialist's job," Colonel Skempton replied, "and any unqualified tinkering could result in a steam explosion down there to add to your other difficulties. As for Doctor Gilvesh, you will remember that that is an observation ward for warm-blooded oxygen-breathers. There is no chlorine available. I'm sorry."

Quietly but firmly, Conway said, "We need supplies of tanked oxygen and chlorine, a nutrient paint sprayer for the Hudlar, a recharging unit for the TLTU's vehicle, and low-residue rations complete with feeding tubes, which will enable the food to be taken without it being exposed to the air of the ward. With the exception of the TLTU's recharger—and I'm sure the team leader would be capable of handling that job if he had step-by-step instructions from one of the maintenance engineers—these items are not bulky. You could move them through the AUGL section and into our lock chamber with probably less trouble than it took getting the DBPK casualty here."

Skempton shook his head. Just as quietly and firmly

he said, "We considered that method of supplying you, Doctor. But we noticed that your lock chamber was left open after the casualty was taken in, and as a result the chamber has been open to contamination for the same period as the rest of the ward. If the lock was cycled to enable us to load it with the needed supplies, water would be drawn in from the AUGL section. When your people pumped out the water to retrieve those supplies, that water, infected with whatever it is that is loose in there, would be returned to the AUGL section, with results we cannot even guess at. I have been told by a number of your colleagues, Doctor, that airborne bacteria can frequently survive and propagate in water.

"Your ward must remain in strict quarantine, Doctor," the Colonel added. "A pathogen that attacks the life-forms not only of its own planet but of four other off-planet species cannot be allowed to get loose. You must realize that as well as I do."

Conway nodded. "There is a possibility that we are overreacting, frightening ourselves unnecessarily because of—"

"A Tralthan FGLI, a Kelgian DBLF, a Melfan ELNT and an Earth-human DBDG became ill to the extent of requiring a mechanical assist with their breathing within a matter of minutes," the Colonel broke in. His expression as he looked at Conway was that of a doctor trying to tell a terminal patient that there was no hope.

Conway felt his face growing red. When he continued he tried to hold his voice steady so as not to appear to be pleading for the impossible. "The effects observed in the ward are totally unlike those experienced on board the *Rhabwar*. We handled and worked with the casualty and a number of DBPK cadavers without suffering any ill effects—"

"Perhaps some Earth-human DBDGs are naturally immune," Skempton broke in. "As far as the hospital is concerned, that is a small consolation."

"Doctor Prilicla and Nurse Naydrad also worked with the DBPKs," said Conway, "unprotected."

"I see," said the Colonel thoughtfully. "A Kelgian

in the ward succumbs while another Kelgian on board the *Rhabwar* escapes. Perhaps there are naturally immune individuals in more than one species, and the *Rhabwar* personnel are fortunate. They, also, are forbidden contact with the hospital or other vessels in the area, although the problem of keeping them supplied is simple compared with yours. But we have thirty hours to work on that one if you conserve your air and—"

"By that time," said the TLTU in unemotional translated tones, "my air will have condensed into water and I shall have long since perished from hypothermia."

"I also," said Gilvesh, without taking its attention from the air hose it was connecting to the Kelgian nurse's neck, "and the bug you are all worried about would not even be interested in a chlorine-breather."

Conway shook his head angrily. "The point I'm trying to make is that we don't know anything at all about this bug."

"Don't you think, Doctor," said O'Mara, in a tone that had the incisive quality of the scalpel Conway had been wielding so recently, "it is high time you found out something about it?"

A long silence followed, while Conway felt his face growing hotter. Then the quiet was diluted by the Hudlar's voice as it directed the transfer team-members in their attempt to make Thornnastor breathe. Conway said sheepishly, "Things *were* a bit hectic for a while, and Thornnastor's analyzer is designed for Tralthan appendages, but I'll see what I can do with it."

"The sooner," said O'Mara caustically, "the better."

Conway disregarded the Chief Psychologist's tone, because O'Mara knew very well what had been happening in the ward and a display of hurt feelings would only waste time. Whatever ultimately happened to the people trapped in the ward, Conway thought, the rest of the warm-blooded oxygen-breathers in the hospital had to be given as much data as possible about the problem, including background information.

As he moved to Thornnastor's analyzer and started

studying the Tralthan control console, Conway began to talk. He described for the people in the ward and the many others outside the search for survivors among the widely scattered wreckage of the DBPK vessel. No doubt Captain Fletcher could, and eventually would, give a more detailed description of the incident, but Conway was concerning himself solely with the medical and physiological aspects.

"The analyzer looks more fearsome than it really is," Murchison's voice explained at one point when he began looking, and feeling, baffled. "The labeled studs have been replaced by tactually coded pads, but the console is organized exactly the same as the one on the *Rhabwar*. I've helped Thorny use that thing on a few occasions. The displays are in Tralthan, of course, but the audio unit is linked to the translator. The air-sample flasks are kept behind the sliding blue panel."

"Thank you," said Conway with feeling, then went on talking about the rescue of the DBPK survivor and the examination and observations that followed. At the same time he cracked the valves of the sample flasks and resealed them after the ward's infection-laden atmosphere rushed in to fill their vacuums. He took samples from distances of a few inches from the patient out to the entry lock at the other end of the ward. Using a suction probe, he took samples from the patient's fur and underlying skin, and surface scrapings from the examination table, used instruments and the ward floor and walls. Then he had to break off to ask Murchison how to load the samples into the analyzer.

Gilvesh used the pause in the narrative to report that the Kelgian nurse's breathing was deep and steady, even though it was the mechanical ventilator that was actually doing the breathing. Prilicla said that Edanelt's condtion remained stable as did Thornnastor's, but at a dangerously low level.

"Get on with it, Conway," O'Mara ordered harshly. "Practically every off-duty medic in the hospital is looking and listening in."

Conway resumed his account of the rescue and retrieval of the injured survivor and the transfer of the cadavers into the *Rhabwar*'s ward, stressing the fact that once inside the ship none of the crew or medical personnel wore masks while handling or examining the single living and several dead DBPKs. Because the survivor remained unconscious and its condition had been deteriorating steadily, the decision had been taken not to prolong the search for other possible survivors. The survey and Cultural Contact cruiser *Descartes* was asked to continue searching the area in case—

"You did *what?*" Colonel Skempton broke in. His face had turned to a sickly gray color.

"The *Descartes* was asked to continue the search of the area for other survivors," Conway replied, "and to gather and study the alien material, books, pictures, personal possessions and so on among the wreckage that might help them understand the new life-form prior to making formal contact. The *Descartes* is one of the few vessels possessing the equipment capable of analyzing the movements of widely dispersed wreckage and of deriving a rough approximation of the wrecked ship's original hyperspatial heading from them. You know the drill, Colonel. The policy in these cases is to backtrack and make contact with the survivor's world as quickly as possible and, if they have been able to find it, to request assistance of a doctor of its own species—"

He broke off because the Colonel was no longer listening to him.

"Priority hypersignal, maximum power," the Colonel was saying to someone off-screen. "Use hospital standby power to boost the service generator. Tell the *Descartes* not, repeat not, to take on board any alien artifacts, technical material or organic specimens from the wreckage. If any such material has already been taken on board they are to jettison it forthwith. On no account is the *Descartes* to seek out and make contact with the wreck's planet of origin, nor is the ship to make physical contact with any other vessel, base, satellite station or subplanetary or planetary body, inhabited or otherwise. They are to proceed at once to Sector General to await further instructions. Radio contact only is allowed. They are expressly forbidden to enter the hospital docking area, and their crew-members will stay on board and will allow no visitors of any species until further notice. Code the signal Federation Emergency. *Move!*"

The Colonel turned to look at Conway again, then continued. "This bug, bacterium, virus, whatever it is, affects warm-blooded oxygen-breathers and perhaps other life-forms as well. As you very well know, Doctor, three-quarters of the citizens of the Federation are warm-blooded oxygen-breathers, with the biggest proportion of those made up of the Kelgian, Tralthan, Melfan and Earth-human life-forms. We stand a good chance of containing the infection here, and of discovering something that might enable us to combat it. But if it hits the *Descartes* it could sweep through the ship so rapidly that they might not be given time to think about the problem, really think it through, before shooting out a distress beacon. Then the ship or ships that go to their aid will carry the infection home—or worse, to other ports of call. An epidemic on such a scale would certainly mean the end of the Federation, and almost certainly the end of civilization on a great many of its worlds.

"We can only hope that the *Descartes* gets the message in time," he added grimly. "With the hospital standby reactor boosting the output of the Corps transmitter, if they don't hear it they have to be deaf, dumb and blind."

"Or very sick," O'Mara observed quietly.

A long silence followed and was broken by the respectful voice of Captain Fletcher.

"If I might make a suggestion, Colonel," he said, "we know the position of the wreckage and of the *Descartes,* if it is still at the disaster site and, very approximately, of the sector that is likely to contain the wrecked ship's home planet. If a distress beacon is released in that area it is almost certain that it will come from the *Descartes.* The *Rhabwar* could answer it, not to give assistance but to warn off any other would-be rescuers."

Obviously the Colonel had forgotten about the ambulance ship. "Are you still connected to the hospital by boarding tube, Captain?" he asked harshly.

"Not since the contamination alert," Fletcher replied. "But if you approve the suggestion we'll need power and consumables for an extended trip. Normally an ambulance ship is gone only for a couple of days at most."

"Approved, and thank you, Captain," said the Colonel. "Arrange for the material to be placed outside your airlock as soon as possible. Your men can load the stores on board later so as to avoid contact with hospital personnel."

Conway had been dividing his attention between the conversation and the analyzer, which looked as if it was about to make a pronouncement. He looked up at the screen and protested: "Colonel, Captain, you can't do that! If you take the *Rhabwar* away we lose Pathologist Murchison and the DBPK specimens, and remove any chance we have of quickly identifying and neutralizing this thing. She is the only pathologist here with first-hand experience of the life-form."

The Colonel looked thoughtful for a moment. "That is a valid objection, Doctor, but consider. There is no dearth of pathologists here at the hospital to help you study the live specimen, even second-hand, and the DBPK cadavers on the *Rhabwar* are staying there. We can contain and, in time, devise some method of treating this disease at the hospital. But the *Rhabwar* could be instrumental in keeping the *Descartes* from infecting the warm-blooded oxygen-breathers of dozens of planets. The original order stands. The *Rhabwar* will refuel and replenish and stand by to answer the expected distress signal from the *Descartes* ... "

He had a lot more to say on the subject of probable future history, including the strong probability of having to place the DBPK patient's home planet and off-world colonies in strict quarantine and to refuse all contact with the new species. The Federation would have to enforce this quarantine in its own defense, and the result might well lead to interstellar war. Then, abruptly, the sound cut out, although it was obvious that Colonel Skempton was still talking to someone off-screen—someone, it was obvious, who was objecting to the *Rhabwar*'s imminent departure as strongly as Conway had.

But the objector, or objectors, was a medical staff-member concerned with solving what was essentially a unique medical problem in extraterrestrial physiology or pharmacology, while Colonel Skempton, like the dedicated Monitor Corps policeman that he was, wanted only to protect a frighteningly large number of innocent bystanders from he knew not what.

Conway looked over at the image of O'Mara. "Sir, I agree that there is the most fearful danger of letting loose a virulent infection that could bring about the collapse of the Federation and cause the technology of many of its individual worlds to slide back into their particular dark ages. But before we react we must first know something about the threat we are reacting against. We must stop and think. Right now we are overreacting and not thinking at all. Could you speak to the Colonel sensibly, sir, and point out to him that a panic reaction frequently does more harm than—"

"Your colleagues are already doing that," the Chief Psychologist replied dryly, "much more forcibly and persuasively than I could, so far without success. But if you feel that we are all guilty of a panic reaction, Doctor, perhaps you will demonstrate the kind of calm, logical reasoning that you think this problem demands?"

Why, you sarcastic . . . Conway raged silently. But before he could speak there was an interruption. Thornnastor's analyzer was displaying bright, incomprehensible symbols on its screen and vocalizing its findings through the translator link.

Analysis of samples one through fifty-three taken in Observation Ward One, AUGL Level, it began tonelessly. *General observations: All atmosphere samples contain oxygen, nitrogen and the usual trace elements in the normal proportions, also small quantities of carbon dioxide, water vapor and chlorine associated with the acceptable levels of leakage from the TLTU life-support system and the Illensan protective suit, and from the expired breaths of the DBDG, DBLF,*

ELNT, FGLI and FROB physiological types, as well as perspiration from the first, second and third of these types. Also present are the phenomes associated with the body odors of the species present who are not wearing overall body protection envelopes, including a hitherto unlisted set, which, by elimination, belongs to the DBPK patient. There are very small quantities of dusts, flakings and fibers abraded from walls, working surfaces and instruments. Some of this material cannot be analyzed without a larger sampling, but it is biochemically inert and harmless. There are also present follicles of Earth-human hair, Kelgian and DBPK fur, flakes of discarded Hudlar nutrient paint, and scales from Tralthan and Melfan tegument.

Conclusion: None of the gases, dusts, colloidal suspensions, bacteria or viruses found in these samples are harmful to any oxygen-breathing life-form.

Without realizing it Conway had been holding his breath, and the inside of his visor misted over briefly as he released it in a short, heavy sigh of disappointment. Nothing. The analyzer could not find anything harmful in the ward.

"I'm waiting, Doctor," said O'Mara.

Conway looked slowly around the ward, at Thornnastor still undergoing artificial respiration, at the Kelgian theater nurse and the spread-eagled Melfan, at the silent Gilvesh and the TLTU hissing quietly in a corner, at the crowded pressure litter and at the beings of several different classifications attached to breathing masks—and found them all looking at him. He thought desperately: Something is loose in here. Something that did not show up in the samples or that the analyzer had classified as harmless anyway. Something that had been harmless, on board the Rhabwar . . .

Aloud, he said, "On the trip back to the hospital we examined and dissected several DBPK cadavers, and thoroughly examined and gave preliminary treatment to the survivor, without body protection and without suffering any ill effects. It is possible that the beings, Earth-human and otherwise, on the Rhabwar all had natural immunity, but that, to my mind, is stretching coincidence beyond its elastic limits. When the survivor was brought into the hospital, protection became necessary because four different physiological types practically dropped in their tracks. We have to ask ourselves, In what way were the circumstances aboard the ambulance ship and in the hospital different?

"We should also ask ourselves," Conway went on, "the question Pathologist Murchison asked after completing her first DBPK dissection, which was, How did a weak, timid and obviously non-aggressive life-form like this one climb to the top of its planet's evolutionary ladder and stay there long enough to develop a civilization capable of interstellar travel? The being is a herbivore. It does not even have the fingernails that are the evolutionary legacy of claws, and it appears to be completely defenseless."

"How about concealed natural weapons?" O'Mara asked. But before Conway could reply, Murchison answered for him.

"No evidence of any, sir," she said. "I paid particular attention to the furless, brownish area of skin at the base of the spine, since this was the only feature of the being's physiology that we did not understand. Both male and female cadavers possessed them. They are small mounds or swellings, four to five inches in diameter and composed of dry, porous tissue. They do not secrete anything and give the appearance of a gland or organ that is inactive or has atrophied. The patches were a uniform pale brown color on the adults. The survivor, who is a female adolescent or pre-adolescent, as far as we can judge, had a pale pink mound, which had been painted to match the coloration of the adult patches."

"Did you analyze the paint?" asked O'Mara.

"Yes, sir," said Murchison. "Some of it had already cracked and flaked off, probably at the time the survivor received its injuries, and we removed the rest of it while we were giving the patient a preoperative cleanup before moving it to the hospital. The paint was organically inert and chemically non-toxic. Giving regard to the patient's age, I assumed that it was a decorative paint applied for cosmetic purposes. Per-

haps the young DBPK was trying to appear more
adult than it actually was."

"Seems a reasonable assumption," said O'Mara.
"So, we have a beastie with natural vanity and no
natural weapons."

Paint, Conway thought suddenly. An idea was stirring at the back of his mind, but he could not make it
take form. Something about paint, or the uses of paint,
perhaps. Decoration, insulation, protection, warning
. . . That must be it—the coating of inert, non-toxic,
harmless paint!

He moved quickly to the instrument rack and withdrew one of the sprayers which a number of e-ts used
to coat their manipulators instead of wearing surgical
gloves. He tested it briefly, because its actuator had
not been designed for DBDG fingers. When he was
sure that he could direct the sprayer with accuracy,
he moved across to the soft, furry and apparently defenseless DBPK patient.

"What the blazes are you doing, Conway?" asked
O'Mara.

"In these circumstances the color of the paint should
not worry the patient too much," Conway said, thinking aloud and ignoring the Chief Psychologist for the
moment. He went on, "Prilicla, will you move closer
to the patient, please. I feel sure there will be a
marked change in its emotional radiation over the next
few minutes."

"I am aware of your feelings, friend Conway," said
Prilicla.

Conway laughed nervously. "In that case, friend
Prilicla, I feel *fairly* sure that I have the answer. But
what about the patient's feelings?"

"Unchanged, friend Conway," said the empath.
"There is a general feeling of concern. It is the same
feeling I detected shortly after it regained consciousness and recovered from its initial fear and confusion.
There is deep concern, sadness, helplessness and . . .
and guilt. Perhaps it is thinking about its friends
who died."

"Its friends, yes," said Conway, switching on the
sprayer and beginning to paint the bare area above

the patient's tail with the bright red inert pigment. "It is worried about its friends who are alive."

The paint dried rapidly and set in a strong, flexible film. By the time Conway had finished spraying on a second layer the patient withdrew its head from underneath its furry tail to look at the repainted patch of bare skin; then it turned its face to Conway and regarded him steadily with its two large, soft eyes. Conway restrained an impulse to stroke its head.

Prilicla made an excited trilling noise, which did not translate, then said, "The patient's emotional radiation shows a marked change, friend Conway. Instead of deep concern and sadness, the predominant emotion is one of intense relief."

That, thought Conway with great feeling, *is my own predominant feeling at the moment.* Aloud, he announced, "That's it, everyone. The contamination emergency is over."

They were all staring at him, and their feelings were so intense and mixed that Prilicla was clinging to the ceiling and shaking as if caught in an emotional gale. Colonel Skempton's face had disappeared from the screen, so it was the craggy features of O'Mara alone glaring out at him.

"Conway," said the Chief Psychologist harshly, "explain."

He began his explanation by requesting a playback of the sound and vision record of the DBPK's treatment from the point a few minutes before it fully regained consciousness. While they were watching Thornnastor, the Kelgian theater nurse and the Melfan Edanelt, who had moved back a short distance to check the patient's air line, Conway said, "The reason why nobody on board the *Rhabwar* was affected during the trip here was that at no time was the patient conscious. Now, the three attending physicians may or may not be handsome to other members of their respective species, but a being, an immature being at that, confronted with them for the first time might well find them visually quite horrendous. Under the circumstances the patient's fear and panic reaction are understandable, but pay particular attention to the

physical response to what, for a few seconds, it regarded as a physical threat.

"The eyes opened wide," he continued as the
scene unfolded on the main screen, "the body stiffened and the chest expanded. A fairly normal reaction, you'll agree. An initial moment of paralysis
followed by hyperventilation so that as much oxygen
as possible is available in the lungs either to scream
for help or to drive the muscles for a quick getaway.
But our attention was concentrated on what was happening to the three attending physicians and the affected team-member, so that we did not notice that the
patient's chest remained expanded for several minutes, that it was, in fact, holding its breath."

On the screen Thornnastor toppled heavily to the
floor, the Kelgian nurse collapsed into a limp heap of
fur, Edanelt's bony undershell clicked loudly against
the floor, the transfer team-member also collapsed and
everyone else who was unprotected headed for the
pressure litter or the breathing masks. "The effects of
this so-called bug," Conway went on, "were sudden
and dramatic. Respiratory failure or partial failure and
collapse, and clear indications that the voluntary
and involuntary muscle systems had been affected.
But there was no rise in body temperature, which
would be expected if the beings concerned were fighting an infection. If infection is ruled out, then the
DBPK life-form was not as defenseless as it
looked . . . "

To be the dominant life-form on its planet, the
DBPKs had to have some means of defending themselves, Conway explained. Or more accurately, the
beings who really needed it had a means of defense.
Probably the adult DBPKs were mentally agile enough
to avoid trouble and to protect their young when
they were small and easily carried. But when the
children grew too large for their parents to protect and
were as yet too inexperienced to protect themselves,
they had evolved a means of defense that was effective
against everything that lived and breathed.

When threatened by natural enemies, the young
DBPKs released a gas—which resembled in its effects

the old Earth-snake venom curare, with the rapidity of action of some of the later nerve gases—so that the enemy's breathing stopped and it was no longer a threat. But it was a two-edged weapon in that it was capable of knocking out everything that breathed oxygen, including the DBPKs themselves. However, the event that triggered the release of the gas also caused the being concerned to hold its breath, which indicated that the toxic material had a complex and unstable molecular structure that broke down and became harmless within a few moments of release, although by that time the natural enemy was no longer a threat.

"With the rise of civilization and the coming of cities, leading to large numbers of the beings of all age groups living closely together, the defense mechanism of the DBPK children became a dangerous embarrassment. A suddenly frightened child, reacting instinctively, could inadvertently kill members of its own family, passers-by in the street or classmates in school. So the organ that released the gas was painted over and sealed until the child reached maturity and the organ became inactive." *There were probably psychological or sociological reasons,* Conway thought, *why the active organs were painted to resemble those of a 'safe' adult.*

"But the patient is a preadolescent of a race that has star travel, and it would expect to see alien life-forms," Conway continued, turning away from the screen as the recording flicked off. "It reacted instinctively because of weakness and physical injury, and almost immediately realized what it had done. Judging by Prilicla's emotion readings, it felt guilty, was desperately sorry for what it had done to some of the friends who had rescued it, and was helpless because it could not warn us of the continuing danger. Now it has been rendered safe again and it is relieved, and judging by its emotional reaction to this situation, I would say that these are nice people—"

Conway broke off as the screen lit again to show the faces of both Colonel Skempton and Major O'Mara. The Colonel looked flustered and embarrassed and he kept his eyes on something he was holding off-screen as he spoke.

"We have received a signal from the *Descartes* within the past few minutes. It reads: *I am disregarding your recent signal. DBPK home planet located and first-contact procedure well advanced. Content of your signal suggests that survivor is a preadolescent DBPK and you are having problems. Warning, do not treat this being without using face masks or light protective suits, or move into the vicinity of the being without similar protection. If precautions have not been taken and hospital personnel are affected, they must be given immediate mechanical assistance with breathing for a period of two-plus hours, after which breathing will resume normally with no aftereffects. This is a natural weapon of defense possessed only by young DBPKs, and the mechanism will be explained to you when the two DBPK medics arrive. They should arrive within four hours in the scoutship* Torrance *to check on the survivor and bring it home. They are also very interested in the multienvironmental hospital idea and have asked permission to return to Sector General for a while to study and . . ."*

All at once it became impossible to hear the Colonel's voice or the *Descartes'* message because Doctor Gilvesh was shouting at Conway and pointing at the Kelgian nurse, whose fur was rippling in frustration because its tracheotomy tube was keeping it from vocalizing. A transfer team-member was also calling to him because Thornnastor was trying to climb to its six elephantine feet while complaining loudly at the indignity of it all. The affected Melfan was also up off the floor and loudly demanding to know what had happened; the Hudlar was shouting that it was hungry; and everyone who had been in the pressure litter began crawling out. The people who had been using masks had discarded them, and they were all trying to make themselves heard to Conway or each other.

Conway swung around to look at the DBPK, suddenly afraid of what the mounting bedlam might be doing to it. There was no longer any danger of their being knocked out by its panic reaction because of the painting exercise he had carried out a few minutes earlier, but the poor thing might be frightened out of its wits.

The DBPK was looking around the ward with its large, soft eyes, but it was impossible to read any expression on its furry, triangular face. Then Prilicla dropped from the ceiling to hover a few inches from Conway's ear.

"Do not feel concern, friend Conway," said the little empath. "Its predominant feeling is curiosity . . . "

Very faintly above the hubbub Conway could hear the series of long blasts on a siren signaling the Contamination All Clear.

PART THREE

Recovery

The two Dwerlan DBPK medics arrived to collect their casualty, but after a brief consultation, decided that the patient was receiving optimum treatment and that they would be grateful if it was allowed to remain there until it could be discharged as fully recovered in two or three weeks' time. Meanwhile, the two visiting medics, whose language had been programed into the translation computer, wandered all over the engineering and medical miracle that was Sector Twelve General Hospital, carrying their tails erect in furry question marks of excitement and pleasure—except, of course, when those large and expressive members were squeezed inside protective suits for environmental reasons.

Several times they visited the ambulance ship, initially to thank the officers and medical team on the *Rhabwar* for saving the young Dwerlan, who had been the only survivor of the disaster to its ship, and later to talk about their impressions of the hospital or of their home world of Dwerla and its four thriving colonies. The visits were welcome breaks in the monotony of what, for the personnel of the *Rhabwar,* had become an extended period of self-education.

At least, that was how the Chief Psychologist described the series of lectures and drills and technical demonstrations that would occupy them for the next few months, unless a distress call was received before then.

"When the ship is in dock you will spend your on-duty time on board," O'Mara had told Conway during one brief but not particularly pleasant interview, "until you have satisfied yourselves, and me, that you are completely familiar with every aspect of your new duty—the ship, its systems and equipment, and something of the specialities of its officers. As much, at least, as they will be expected to learn about your specialty. Right now, and in spite of having to answer two distress calls in as many weeks, you are still ignorant.

"Your first mission resulted in considerable inconvenience to yourselves," he had gone on sourly, "and the second in a near panic for the hospital. But neither job could be called a challenge either to your extraterrestrial medical skill or Fletcher's e-t engineering expertise. The next mission may not be so easy, Conway. I suggest you prepare yourselves for it by learning to act together as a team, and not by fighting continually to score points like two opposing teams. And don't bang the door on your way out."

And so it was that the *Rhabwar* became a ship-shaped classroom and laboratory in which the ship's officers lectured on their specialties in as much detail as they considered mere medical minds could take, and the medical team tried to teach them the rudiments of e-t physiology. Because so many of the lectures had to give a general, rather than a too narrowly specialized, treatment of their subjects, it was usually the Captain or Conway who delivered them. With the exception of the watch-keeping officer on duty in Control —and he could look and listen in and ask questions —all the ship's officers were present at the medical lectures.

On this occasion Conway was discussing e-t comparative physiology.

" . . . Unless you are attached to a multienvironment hospital like this one," Conway was explaining to Lieutenants Haslam, Chen and Dodds, and with a brief glance at the vision pickup to include Captain Fletcher in Control, "you normally meet extraterrestrials one species at a time, and refer to them by their planet of origin. But here in the hospital and in the wrecked ships we will encounter, rapid and accurate identification of incoming patients and rescued survivors is vital, because all too often the casualties are in no fit condition to furnish physiological information about themselves. For this reason we have evolved a four-letter physiological classification system, which works like this:

"The first letter denotes the level of physical evolution," he continued. "The second letter indicates the type and distribution of limbs and sensory equipment, which in turn gives us information regarding the positioning of the brain and the other major organs. The remaining two letters refer to the combination of metabolism and gravity and/or atmospheric-pressure requirements of the being, and these are tied in with the physical mass and the protective tegument, skin, fur, scales, osseous plating and so on represented by the relevant letter.

"It is at this point during the hospital lectures," Conway said, smiling, "that we have to remind some of our e-t medical students that the initial letter of their classifications should not be allowed to give them feelings of inferiority, and that the level of physical evolution, which is, of course, an adaptation to their planetary environment, has no relation to the level of intelligence . . . "

Species with the prefix A, B or C, he went on to explain, were water-breathers. On most worlds, life had originated in the sea, and these beings had developed high intelligence without having to leave it. The letters D through F were warm-blooded oxygen-breathers, into which group fell most of the intelligent races in the Galaxy; and the G to K types were also warm-blooded but insectile. The L's and M's were light-gravity, winged beings.

Chlorine-breathing life-forms were contained in the O and P groups, and after that came the more exotic, the more highly evolved physically and the downright weird types. These included the ultra-high-temperature and frigid-blooded or crystalline beings, and entities capable of modifying their physical structures at will. Those possessing extrasensory powers sufficiently well developed to make ambulatory or manipulatory appendages unnecessary were given the prefix V, regardless of physical size or shape.

" . . . There are anomalies in the system," Conway went on, "but these can be blamed on a lack of imagination by its originators. One of them was the AACP life-form, which has a vegetable metabolism. Normally, the prefix A denotes a water-breather, there being nothing lower in the system than the piscine life-forms. But then we discovered the AACPs, who were, without doubt, vegetable intelligences, and the plant came before the fish—"

"Control here. Sorry for the interruption, Doctor."

"You have a question, Captain?" asked Conway.

"No, Doctor. Instructions. Lieutenants Haslam and Dodds to Control and Lieutenant Chen to the Power Room, at once. Casualty Deck, we have a distress call, physiological classification unknown. Please ensure maximum readiness—"

"We're always ready," said Naydrad, its fur bristling in irritation.

"Pathologist Murchison and Doctor Conway, come to Control as soon as convenient."

As the three Monitor Corps officers disappeared rapidly up the ladder of the central well, Murchison said, "You realize, of course, that this means we will probably not be given the Captain's second lecture on control-system organization and identification in vessels of non-bifurcate extraterrestrials this afternoon." She laughed suddenly. "I am not an empath like Prilicla here, but I detect an overall feeling of relief."

Naydrad made an untranslatable noise, which was possibly a subdued cheer in Kelgian.

"I also feel," she went on, "that our Captain is merely being polite. He wants to see us up there as soon as possible."

"Everybody," said Prilicla as it began checking the e-t instrument packs, "wants to be an empath, friend Murchison."

They arrived in Control slightly breathless after their climb up the gravity-free well past the five intervening decks. Murchison had considerably more breath available than Conway, even though she had used a lot of it telling him that he was running to adipose and that his center of gravity was beginning to drop below his waistline—something that had not happened to the delightfully top-heavy pathologist over the years. As they straightened up, looking around the small, darkened compartment and at the intent faces lit only by indicator lights and displays, Captain Fletcher motioned them into the two supernumerary positions and waited for them to strap in before he spoke.

"We were unable to obtain an accurate fix on the distress beacon," he began without preamble, "because of distortion caused by stellar activity in the area, a small cluster whose stars are in an early and very active period of evolution. But I expect the signal has been received by other and much closer Corps installations, who will obtain a more accurate fix, which they will relay to the hospital before we make the first Jump. For this reason I intend proceeding at one instead of four-G thrust to Jump-distance, losing perhaps half an hour, in the hope of obtaining a closer fix, which would save time, a great deal of time, when we reach the disaster site. Do you understand?"

Conway nodded. On many occasions he had been awaiting a subspace radio message, usually in answer to a request for environmental information regarding a patient whose physiological type was new to the hospital, and the signal had been well-nigh unreadable because of interference from intervening stellar objects. The hospital's receptors were the equal of those used by the major Monitor Corps bases, and were hundreds of times more sensitive than any equipment mounted in a ship. If any sort of message carrying the co-ordinates of the distressed vessel's position was received by Sector General, it would be filtered and deloused and relayed to the ambulance ship within seconds.

Always provided, of course, that their ship had not already left normal space.

"Is anything known about the disaster area?" asked Conway, trying to hide his irritation at being treated as a complete ignoramus in all matters outside his medical specialty. "Nearby planetary systems, perhaps, whose inhabitants might have some knowledge regarding the physiology of the survivors, if any?"

"In this kind of operation," said the Captain, "I did not think there would be time to go looking for the survivors' friends."

Conway shook his head. "You'd be surprised, Captain," he said. "In the hospital's rescue experience, if the initial disaster does not kill everyone within the first few minutes, the ship's safety devices can keep the survivors alive for several hours or even days. Furthermore, unless faced with a surgical emergency, it is better and safer to institute palliative treatment on a completely strange life-form and if it can be found, send for the being's own doctor, as we would have done with the Dwerlan casualty had its injuries been less serious. There may even be times when it is better to do nothing at all for the patient and allow its own healing processes to proceed without interruption."

Fletcher started to laugh, thought better of it when he realized that Conway was serious, then began tapping buttons on his console. In the big astrogation cube at the center of the control room there appeared a three-dimensional star chart with a fuzzy red spot at its center. There were about twenty stars in the volume of space represented by the projection, three of which were joined and enclosed by motionless swirls and tendrils of luminous material.

"That fuzzy spot," said the Captain apologetically, "should be a point of light signifying the position of the distressed ship. As it is, we know its whereabouts only to the nearest hundred million miles. The area has not been surveyed or even visited by Federation ships, because we would not expect to find inhabited systems in a star cluster that is at such an early stage in its formation. In any case, the present position of the distressed ship does not indicate that it is native to the area, unless it malfunctioned soon after Jumping. But a closer study of the probabilities—"

"What bothers me," said Murchison quickly as she sensed another highly specialized lecture coming on, "is why more of our distressed aliens are not rescued by their own people. That rarely happens."

"True, ma'am," Fletcher replied. "A few cases have been recorded where we found technologically interesting wrecks and a few odds and ends—the equivalent of e-t pin-ups, magazines, that sort of thing —but there were no dead e-ts. Their bodies and those of the survivors, if any, had been taken away. It is odd, but thus far we have found no civilized species that does not show respect for its dead. Also, do not forget that a space disaster is a fairly rare occurrence for a single star-traveling species, and any rescue mission they could mount would probably be too little and too late. But to the Galaxy-wide, multispecies Federation, space accidents are not rare. They are expected. Our reaction time to any disaster is very fast because ships like this one are constantly on standby; and so we tend to get there first.

"But we were discussing the difficulties of establishing the original course constants of a wrecked ship," the Captain went on, refusing to be sidetracked from his lecture. "First, there is the fact that a detour is frequently necessary to reach the destination system. This is because of pockets of unusual stellar density, black holes and similar normal-space obstructions that cause dangerous areas of distortion in the hyperspace medium, so very few ships are able to reach their destinations in fewer than five Jumps. Second, there are the factors associated with the size of the distressed ship and the number of its hypergenerators. A small vessel with one generator poses fewest problems. But if the ship is similar in mass to ourselves, and we carry a matched pair, or if it is a very large ship requiring four or six hypergenerators . . . Well, it would then depend on whether the generators went out simultaneously or consecutively.

"Our ships and, presumably, theirs," Fletcher continued, warming to his subject, "are fitted with safety cutoffs to all generators, should one fail. But those safety devices are not always foolproof, because it takes only a split-second delay in shutting down a generator and the section of the ship structurally associated with it pops into normal space, tearing free of the rest of the vessel and in the process imparting an unbalanced braking motion, which sends the ship spinning off at a tangent to its original course. The shock to the vessel's structure would probably cause the other generator or generators to fail, and the process would be repeated, so that a series of such events occurring within a few seconds in hyperspace could very well leave the wreckage of the distressed ship strung out across a distance of several light-years. That is the reason why—"

He broke off as an attention signal flashed on his panel. "Astrogation, sir," Lieutenant Dodds announced briskly. "Five minutes to Jump."

"Sorry, ma'am," said the Captain. "We will have to continue this discussion at another time. Power Room, status report, please."

"Both hypergenerators at optimum, and output matched within the safety limits, sir," came Chen's reply.

"Life-support?"

"Systems also optimum," Chen said. "Artificial gravity on all deck levels at one-G Earth-normal setting. Zero-G in the central well, generator housings and in the Cinrusskin doctor's quarters."

"Communications?"

"Still nothing from the hospital, sir," Haslam replied.

"Very well," said the Captain. "Power Room, shut down the thrusters, and stand by to abort the Jump until minus one minute." In an aside to Murchison and Conway he explained: "During the final minute we're committed to the Jump, whether a signal comes from the hospital or not."

"Killing thrusters," said Chen. "Acceleration zero and standing by."

There was a barely detectable surge as the ship's

acceleration ceased and the one-G was maintained by the deck's artificial-gravity grids. A display on the Captain's panel marked off the minutes and the seconds in a silence that was broken only by a quiet sigh from Fletcher as the figures marched into the final minute, then the final thirty seconds . . .

"Communications, sir!" said Haslam quickly. "Signal from Sector General, amended co-ordinates for the distress beacon. No other message."

"They certainly didn't leave themselves time for a tender farewell," said the Captain with a nervous laugh. Before he could continue, the Jump gong sounded and the ambulance ship and its occupants moved into a self-created universe where action and reaction were not equal and velocities were not limited to the speed of light.

Instinctively, Conway's eyes went to the direct-vision port and beyond it to the inner surface of the flickering gray globe that enclosed the ship. At first the surface appeared to be a featureless and absolutely smooth gray barrier, but gradually a sensation of depth, of far too much depth, became apparent and an ache grew behind his eyes as they tried to cope with the twisting, constantly changing gray perspectives.

A maintenance engineer at the hospital had once told him that in hyperspace, material things, whether their atomic or molecular building blocks were arranged into the shapes of people or hardware, had no physical existence; that it was still not clearly understood by the physicists why it was that at the conclusion of a Jump the ship, its equipment and its occupants did not materialize as a homogenous molecular stew. The fact that such a thing had never happened before, as far as the engineer knew, did not mean that it could not happen, and could the doctor suggest a really strong sedative that would keep the engineer non-existently asleep while he was Jumping home on his next leave?

Smiling to himself at the memory, Conway looked away from the twisting grayness. Inside Control the non-existent officers were concentrating all their attention on panels and displays that had no philosophical reality while they recited the esoteric litanies of their profession. Conway looked at Murchison, who nodded, and they both unstrapped and stood up.

The Captain stared at them as if he had forgotten they were there. "Naturally you will have things to do, ma'am, Doctor. The Jump will last just under two hours. If anything interesting happens I'll relay it to you on the Casualty Deck screen."

They pulled themselves aft along the ladder of the gravity-free well, and a few seconds later, staggered slightly as they stepped onto the Casualty Deck. Its one-G of artificial gravity reminded them that there was such a thing as up and down. The level was empty, but they could see the spacesuited figure of Naydrad through the airlock view panel as it stood on the wing where it joined the hull.

That particular section of wing was fitted with artificial-gravity grids to aid in the maneuvering of awkward loads into and out of the airlock, which was why the Kelgian charge nurse appeared to be standing horizontally on the, to them, vertical wall of the wing. It saw them and waved before resuming its testing of the airlock and wing exterior lighting system.

In addition to the artificial gravity holding it to the wing surface two safety lines were attached to Naydrad's suit. A person who became detached from its ship in hyperspace was lost, more utterly and completely lost than anyone could really imagine.

The Casualty Deck's equipment and medication had already been checked by Naydrad and Prilicla, but Conway was required to give everything a final checkout. Prilicla, who needed more rest than its much less fragile colleagues, was in its cabin, and Naydrad was busy outside. This meant that Conway could check their work without Prilicla pretending to ignore him and Naydrad rippling its fur in disapproval.

"I'll check the pressure litter first," said Conway.

"I'll help you," offered Murchison, "and with the ward medication stores downstairs. I'm not tired."

"As you very well know," said Conway as he opened the panel of the litter's stowage compartment, "the proper term is 'on the lower deck,' not 'downstairs.' Are you trying to give the Captain the idea that you are ignorant in everything but your own specialty?"

Murchison laughed quietly. "He seems already to have formed that idea, judging by the insufferably patronizing way he talks, or rather lectures, to me." She helped him roll out the litter, then added briskly: "Let's inflate the envelope with an inert at triple Earth-normal pressure, just in case we get a heavy-gravity casualty this time. Then we can brew up a few likely atmospheres."

Conway nodded and stepped back as the thin but immensely tough envelope ballooned outwards. Within a few seconds it had grown so taut that it resembled a thin, elongated glass dome enclosing the upper surface of the litter. The internal pressure indicator held steady.

"No leaks," Conway reported, switching on the pump that would extract and recompress the inert gas in the envelope. "We'll try the Illensan atmosphere next. Mask on, just in case."

The base of the litter had a storage compartment in which were racked the basic surgical instruments, the glove extensions that would enable treatment to be carried out on a casualty without the doctor having to enter the envelope, and general-purpose filter masks for several different physiological types. He handed a mask to Murchison and donned one himself. "I still think you should try harder to give the impression that you are intelligent as well as beautiful."

"Thank you, dear," Murchison replied, her voice muffled by the mask. She watched Conway use the mixing controls for a moment, checking that the corrosive yellow fog that was slowly filling the envelope was, in fact, identical to the atmosphere used by the chlorine-breathing natives of Illensa.

"Ten, even five years ago, that may have been true," she went on. "It was said that every time I put on a lightweight suit I upped the blood pressure, pulse and respiration rate of every non-geriatric male

DBDG in the hospital. It was mostly you who said it, as I remember."

"You still have that effect on Earth-human DBDGs, believe me," said Conway, briefly offering his wrist so that she could check his pulse. "But you should concentrate on impressing the ship's officers with your intellect; otherwise, I shall have too much competition and the Captain will consider you prejudicial to discipline. Or maybe we are being a bit too unfair to the Captain. I heard one of the officers talking about him, and it seems that he was one of the Monitor Corps' top instructors and researchers in extraterrestrial engineering. When the special ambulance ship project was first proposed, the Cultural Contact people placed him first as their choice for ship commander.

"In some ways he reminds me of one of our diagnosticians," Conway went on, "with his head stuffed so full of facts that he can only communicate in short lectures. So far, Corps discipline, the respect due his rank and professional ability have enabled him to operate effectively without interpersonal communication in depth. But now he has to learn to talk to ordinary people—people, that is, who are not subordinates or fellow officers—and sometimes he does not do a very good job of it. But he is trying, however, and we must—"

"I seem to remember," Murchison broke in, "a certain young and very new intern who was a lot like that. In fact, O'Mara still insists that this person prefers the company of his extraterrestrial colleagues to those of his own species."

"With one notable exception," Conway said smugly.

Murchison squeezed his arm affectionately and said that she could not react to that remark as she would have liked while wearing a mask and coveralls, and that it was becoming increasingly difficult to concentrate on Conway's checklist as time went on. But the high level of emotional radiation in the area was reduced suddenly by the Jump gong signaling the ship's return to normal space.

The Casualty Deck's screen remained blank, but Fletcher's voice came from the speaker a few seconds

later. *"Control here. We have returned to normal space
close to the position signaled by the beacon, but there
is as yet no sign of a distressed ship or wreckage.
However, since it is impossible to achieve pinpoint accuracy with a hyperspatial Jump, the distressed vessel
could be many millions of miles away . . ."*

"He's lecturing again," Murchison sighed.

*". . . but the impulses from our sensors travel at
the velocity of light and are reflected back at the same
speed. This means that if ten minutes elapsed before
we registered a contact, the distance of the object
would be half that time in seconds multiplied by
the—"*

"Contact, sir!"

*"I stand corrected, not too many millions of miles.
Very well. Astrogation, give me the distance and
course constants, please. Power Room, stand by for
maximum thrust in ten minutes. Charge Nurse Naydrad, cancel your EVA immediately. Casualty Deck,
you will be kept informed. Control out."*

Conway returned his attention to the pressure litter,
evacuating the chlorine atmosphere and replacing it
with the high-pressure superheated steam breathed by
the TLTU life-forms. He had begun to check the litter's thrusters and attitude controls when Naydrad
slithered through the inner lock seal, its suit beaded
with condensation and still radiating the cold of outside. The charge nurse watched them for a few moments, then said that if it was needed it would be in its
cabin thinking beautiful thoughts.

They checked the compartment's restraints with
great care. From experience Conway knew that extraterrestrial casualties were not always co-operative, and
some of them could be downright aggressive when
strange, to them, beings began probing them with
equally strange devices of unknown purpose. For that
reason the compartment was fitted with a variety of
material and immaterial restraints in the forms of
straps, webbing, and tractor- and pressor-beam pro-
jectors sufficient to immobilize anything up to the
mass and muscle power of a Tralthan in the final
stages of its premating dance. Conway devoutly hoped

that the restraints would never be needed, but they
were available and had to be checked.

Two hours passed before any news was forthcoming
from the Captain. Then it was brief and to the point.

*"Control here. We have established that the con-
tact is not a naturally occurring interstellar body. We
will close with it in seventy-three minutes."*

"Time enough," said Conway, "to check the ward
medication."

A section of the floor of the Casualty Deck opened
downwards onto the deck below, which was divided
into a ward and a combination laboratory-pharmacy.
The ward was capable of accommodating ten casualties of reasonably normal mass—Earth-human size
and below—and of producing a wide range of environmental life-support. In the laboratory section,
which was separated from the ward by a double airlock, were stored the constituent gases and liquids used
by every known life-form in the Galactic Federation
and with the capability, it was hoped, of reproducing
atmospheres of those yet unknown. The lab also contained sets of specialized surgical instruments capable
of penetrating the teguments of and performing curative surgery on the majority of the Federation's
physiological types.

The pharmacy section was stocked with the known
specifics against the more common e-t diseases and
abnormal conditions—in small quantities because of
limitations of space—together with the basic analysis
equipment common to any e-t pathology lab. All this
meant that there was very little space for two people
to work, but then Conway had never complained
about working closely with Murchison and vice versa.

They had barely finished checking the e-t instru-
ments when Fletcher's voice returned, and before the
Captain had finished speaking they were joined by
Prilicla and Naydrad.

*"Control here. We have visual acquisition of the
distressed vessel, and the telescope is locked on with
full magnification. You can see what we can see. We
are decelerating and will halt approximately fifty meters from the vessel in twelve minutes. During the last*

*few minutes of our approach, I propose using my
tractor beams at low intensity to check the spin of the
distressed ship. Comments, Doctor?"*

The shape on the screen appeared at first to be a
pale, circular blur against the background luminosity
associated with the nearby star cluster. Only after a
few seconds of close examination of the image did it
become apparent that the blurred circle was, in fact, a
thick metallic-gray disk that was spinning like a tossed
coin. Apart from three slight protuberances spaced
equally around the circumference of the disk, there
were no other obvious features. As Conway and the
others stared the spinning ship grew larger, overflow-
ing the edges of the screen until magnification was
stepped down and they could once again see the vessel whole.

Clearing his throat, Conway said, "I should be careful while checking the spin, Captain. There is at
least one species we know of which requires constant
spin on their space and other vehicles to maintain
life-support—"

*"I'm familiar with the technology of the Rollers of
Drambo, Doctor. They are a species which must roll,
either naturally while traveling over the surface of
their world or artificially if operating otherwise station-
ary machines, if their vital life-functions are to continue. They do not possess a heart as such, but use a
gravity-feed system to maintain circulation of the
blood, so that to stop rolling for more than a few seconds means death to them.*

*"But this ship is not spinning around its vertical,
lateral or longitudinal axis. In my opinion it is tumbling in a completely uncontrolled fashion, and its spin
should be checked. Rather, it must be checked if we
are to gain rapid entry to the ship and to its survivors,
if any. But you're the doctor, Doctor."*

For Prilicla's sake Conway tried hard to control his
irritation. "Very well. Check the spin, Captain, but
carefully. You wouldn't want to place an additional
and unnecessary strain on the already damaged and
weakened fabric of the ship, or cause wreckage to
shift onto possible survivors, or to open a seam that

might cause a lethal pressure drop in the vessel's atmosphere."

"Control out."

"You know, if you two stopped trying to impress each other with how much you know about the other person's job," Murchison said seriously, "Doctor Prilicla would not get the shakes so often."

On the screen the magnification was stepped down again as the ambulance ship closed with the distressed vessel, whose rate of spin was slowing under the tangential pull of the *Rhabwar*'s tractors. By the time both ships were motionless with respect to each other at a distance of fifty meters, the alien vessel had already presented its upper and lower surfaces for detailed inspection by eye and camera. One fact among many was glaringly obvious. But before Conway could comment on it, Control got there first.

"The distressed vessel appears to have retained its structural integrity, Doctor. There are no indications of external damage or malfunction, no signs of external substructures or antenna systems carried away or sheared off. Preliminary sensor analysis of the hull surface shows temperature variations with the highest readings in the areas of the bulges on the ship's rim. These three areas are also emitting residual radiation of the type associated with hyperdrive field generation. There is evidence of a major power concentration positioned around the central hub of the vessel, and several subconcentrations of power, all of which appear to be linked together by a system of power lines which are still active. The details are on the schematic . . ."

The picture of the alien ship was replaced by a plan view diagram showing the positions and intensities of the power concentrations in shades of red, with yellow dotted lines indicating the connecting power lines. The original image returned.

" . . . There is no evidence of leakage of a gas or fluid which might constitute the atmosphere used by the crew, and neither, up to the present, can I detect a method of entry into the ship. There are no airlocks, either cargo or personnel, nor any of the markings as-

sociated with entry and exit points, inspection and maintenance panels, replenishment points for consumables. In fact, there are no markings or insignia or instructions or warning signs visible at all. The ship is finished in bare, polished metal, as far as we can see, and the only color variation is caused by different alloys being used in certain areas."

"No paint scheme or insignias," said Naydrad, edging closer to the screen. "Have we at last discovered a species completely devoid of vanity?"

"Perhaps the visual equipment of the species is in question," Prilicla added. "They may simply be color blind."

"The reason is more likely to be aerodynamic than physiological."

"As far as we are concerned," Conway joined in, "the reason is much more likely to be medical when the crew of a seemingly undamaged ship releases a distress beacon. Whatever the reason, the condition of the occupants is likely to be grave. We must go over there at once, Captain."

"I agree. Lieutenant Dodds will remain in Control. Haslam and Chen will accompany me to the ship. I suggest you wear heavy-duty suits because of their longer duration. Our primary objective is to find a way inside, and that could take some time. What are your intentions, Doctor?"

"Pathologist Murchison will remain here," Conway replied. "Naydrad will suit up as you suggest and stand by with the litter outside the airlock, and Prilicla and I will accompany you to the ship. But I shall wear a lightweight suit with extra air tanks. Its gauntlets are thinner and I may have to treat survivors."

"I understand. Meet at the lock in fifteen minutes."

The conversation of the party investigating the alien ship would be relayed to the Casualty Deck and recorded by Dodds in Control, and the three-view projection of the vessel would be updated as new data became available. But when they were in the *Rhabwar*'s lock and about to launch themselves towards the other ship, Fletcher touched helmets with Conway—

signifying that he wanted to talk without being overheard on the suit radio frequency.

"I am having second thoughts about the number
of people making the initial investigation and entry,"
the Captain said, his voice muffled and distorted by
its passage through the fabric of their helmets. "A certain amount of caution is indicated here. That ship appears to be undamaged and operational. It occurred
to me that the crew rather than the ship are in a distressed condition and that their problem might be psychological rather than medical—they might be in a
disturbed and non-rational state. So much so that they
may react badly and possibly Jump if too many
strange creatures started clambering all over their
hull."

Now he has delusions of being a xenopsychologist!
Conway thought. "You have a point, Captain. But
Prilicla and I will not clamber, we will look carefully
and touch nothing without first reporting what we have
found."

They began by examining the underside of the disk-
shaped vessel. It had to be the underside, Fletcher insisted, because there were four propulsion orifices
grouped closely around its diametrical center. He was
pretty sure the holes were the mouths of jet venturis
because of the heat discoloration and pitting that surrounded them. From the position and direction of the
thrusters it was clear that the ship's direction of travel
was along its vertical axis, although the Captain
thought that it would be able to skim edge on for aerodynamic maneuvering in an atmosphere.

In addition to the burned areas around the jet orifices there was a large, circular patch of roughened
metal centered on the underside and extending out to
approximately one quarter of the ship's radius. There
were numerous other roughened areas, only a few
inches across for the most part and of various shapes
and sizes, scattered over the underside and around the
rim. These rough areas puzzled Fletcher because they
were really rough—rough enough to snag his gauntlets
and pose a danger to anyone wearing a lightweight
suit. But he was chiefly puzzled because the rest of the

ship looked as if it had been put together by watch-makers.

There were three rough areas which corresponded with the swellings on the rim of the vessel and which were almost certainly the housings of its hypergenera-tors.

When they moved to the upper surface they found more tiny blemishes, raised very slightly above the surrounding surface, which seemed to be some kind of imperfection in the metal plating. Fletcher said they reminded him of corrosion incrustations except for the fact that there was no difference between their color and the color of the metal they had attacked.

Nowhere was there any evidence of transparent material being used in the ship's construction. None of its communications antennae or sensory receptors had been deployed, so, presumably, this equipment had been retracted before the distress beacon had been re-leased, and was concealed below some of the ship's incredibly well fitting access panels and covers—a few of which had been distinguishable only because of slight color differences in the metal panels and the surrounding hull plating. After searching and straining their eyes for nearly two hours, they still found no sign of anything resembling an external actuator for any of these panels. The ship was locked up tight, and the Captain could give no estimate of the time needed to effect an entry.

"This is supposed to be a rescue attempt and not a leisurely scientific investigation." Conway sounded exasperated. "Can we force an entry?"

"Only as a last resort," the Captain replied. "We do not want to risk offending the inhabitants until we are sure their condition is desperate. We will concentrate our search for an entry port on the rim. The flat, disk-like configuration of the ship, which presents its upper surface to the direction of travel, suggests that its crew would enter via the rim. Its upper surface should, I feel sure, contain the control and living compartments and, hopefully, the survivors."

"Right," agreed Conway. "Prilicla, concentrate your

empathic faculty topside while we search the rim. Again."

The minutes flew by without anyone reporting anything but negative results. Impatiently, Conway guided his suit along the edge of the rim until he was hanging just a few meters from Prilicla's position topside. On impulse, he energized his boot and wrist magnets, and when they had pulled him gently against the hull, he freed one foot and kicked hard against the metal plating three times.

Immediately, the suit frequency went into a howl of oscillation as everyone tried to report noise and vibration in their sensor pads at the same time. When silence had returned, Conway spoke.

"Sorry. I should have warned you I was going to do that," he said, knowing that if he had done so there would have been an interminable argument with the Captain, ending in refusal of permission. "We're using up too much time. This is a rescue mission, dammit, and we don't even know if there is anyone to rescue. Some kind of response is needed from inside the ship. Prilicla, did we get anything?"

"No, friend Conway," said the emptah. "There is no response to your striking the hull, and no evidence of conscious mentating or emoting. But I cannot yet be sure that there are no survivors. I have the feeling that the total emotional radiation in the vicinity of the ship is not made up solely by the four Earth-humans present and myself."

"I see," said Conway. "In your usual polite and self-effacing fashion you are telling us that we are stirring up too much emotional mud and that we should clear the area so that you can work without interference. How much distance will you need, Doctor?"

"If everyone moves back to the hull of our ship," said Prilicla, "that would be more than adequate, friend Conway. It would also assist me if they engaged in cerebral rather than emotional thinking, and switched off their suit radios."

For what seemed to be a very long time they stood together on the wing of the *Rhabwar* with their backs to the alien ship and Prilicla. Conway had told them that if they were to watch the empath at work they would probably feel anxiety or impatience or disappointment if it did not find a survivor quickly, and any kind of strong feeling would cause emotional interference as far as Prilicla was concerned. Conway did not know what form of cerebral exercise the others were performing to clear their minds of troublesome emotional radiation, but he decided to look around him at the star clusters embedded in their billows and curtains of glowing star stuff. Then the thought came that he was exposing his eyes and his mind to too much sheer splendor, and the feeling of wonder might also be disturbing to an emotion-sensitive.

Suddenly the Captain, who had been sneaking an occasional look at Prilicla, began pointing towards the other ship. Conway switched on his radio in time to hear Fletcher say, "I think we can start emoting again."

Conway swung round to see the spacesuited figure of Prilicla hanging above the metal landscape of the ship like a tiny moon while it directed a spray of fluorescent marker paint at an area midway between the center and the rim. The painted area was already about three meters across and the empath was still extending it.

"Prilicla?" called Conway.

"Two sources, friend Conway," the Cinrusskin reported. "Both are so faint that I cannot pinpoint them with any degree of accuracy other than to say they are somewhere beneath the marked area of hull. The emotional radiation in both cases is characteristic of the unconscious and severely weakened subject. I would say they are in worse shape than the Dwerlan we rescued recently. They are very close to death."

Before Conway could reply, the Captain said harshly, "Right, that's it. Haslam, Chen, break out the portable airlock and cutting gear. This time we'll search the rim in pairs, except for Doctor Prilicla, with one man doing the looking with his light switched off while the other directs side lighting onto the plating so as to throw any joins into relief. Try to find anything that looks like a lock entrance, and cut a way in if we can't solve the combination. Search carefully but quickly. If we can't find a way through the rim inside half an hour, we'll cut through the upper hull in the center of the marked area and hope we don't hit any control linkages or power lines. Have you anything to add, Doctor?"

"Yes," said Conway. "Prilicla, is there anything else, anything at all, you can tell me about the condition of the survivors?"

He was already on the way back to the distressed ship with the Captain slightly ahead of him, and the little empath had attached itself magnetically to the marked area of hull.

"My data is largely negative, friend Conway," said Prilicla, "and comprises supposition rather than fact. Neither being is registering pain, but both share feelings suggesting starvation, asphyxiation and the need of something that is vital to the continuance of life. One of the beings is trying very hard to stay alive while the other appears merely to be angry. The emotional radiation is so tenuous that I cannot state with certainty that the beings are intelligent life-forms, but the indications are that the angry one is probably a nonintelligent lab animal or ship's pet. These are little more than guesses, friend Conway, and I could be completely wrong."

"I doubt that," said Conway. "But those feelings of starvation and strangulation puzzle me. The ship is undamaged, so food and air supplies should be available."

"Perhaps, friend Conway," Prilicla replied timidly, "they are in the terminal stages of a respiratory disease, rather than suffering from gross physical injury."

"In which case," said Murchison, joining the conversation from the *Rhabwar*, "I will be expected to brew up something efficacious against a dose of extraterrestrial pneumonia. Thank *you*, Doctor Prilicla!"

The portable airlock—a fat, lightweight metal cylinder swathed in the folds of transparent plastic that would form its antechamber—was positioned close to the alien ship. While Prilicla remained as physically close as possible to the survivors, Chen and Haslam joined the Captain and Conway in a final search for a fine line on the rim plating that might enclose an entry port.

He tried to be thorough without wasting time, because Prilicla did not think there was any time to waste as far as the two survivors were concerned. But the ship was close to eighty meters in diameter and they had an awful lot of rim to search in half an hour. Still, there had to be a way in, and their main problem was that, despite the many rough and incrusted patches, the ship's structure represented an incredibly fine piece of precision engineering.

"Is it possible," Conway asked suddenly, "that the reason for the ship's distress is these rough patches?" The side of his helmet was close to the hull as he directed his spotlight at an acute angle onto the area that Fletcher was scanning for joins. "Perhaps the troubles of the survivors are a secondary effect. Maybe the unnaturally tight fit of the plating and panels is meant as a protection against attack by some kind of galloping corrosion native to the survivors' home planet."

There was a lengthy silence, then Fletcher said, "That is a very disquieting idea, Doctor, especially since your galloping corrosion might infect our ship. But I don't think so. The incrusted patches appear to be made of the same material as the underlying metal and not a coating of corrosion. As well, they appear to avoid rather than attack the joins."

Conway did not reply. At the back of his mind an idea had begun to stir and take shape, but it dissolved abruptly as Chen's voice sounded excitedly in his phones.

"Sir, over here!"

Chen and Haslam had found what seemed to be a large, circular hatch or section of plating approximately a meter in diameter, and they were already spraying the circumference with marker paint when Fletcher, Prilicla and Conway arrived. There were no rough patches inside the circular line or outside it except for two tiny rough spots set side by side just beyond the lower edge of the circle. Closer examination showed a five-inch-diameter circle enclosing the two rough patches.

"That," said Chen, trying hard to control his excitement, "could be some kind of actuator control for the hatch."

"You're probably right," said the Captain. "Good work, both of you. Now, set up the portable lock around this hatch. Quickly." He placed his sensor plate against the metal. "There is a large empty space behind this hatch, so it is almost certainly an entry lock. If we can't open it manually we'll cut our way in."

"Prilicla?" called Conway.

"Nothing, friend Conway," said the empath. "The survivors' radiation is much too faint to be detectable above the other sources in the area."

"Casualty Deck," Conway said. When Murchison responded, he went on quickly: "Considering the condition of the survivors, would you mind coming over here with the portable analyzer? Atmosphere samples will be available shortly. It would save some time if we didn't have to send them to you for analysis, and shorten the time needed to prepare the litter for the casualties."

"I was expecting you to think of that," Murchison replied briskly. "Ten minutes."

Conway and the Captain ignored the loose folds of transparent fabric and the light-alloy seal that bumped weightlessly against their backs while Haslam and Chen drew the material into position around the entry lock and attached it to the hull with instant sealant. Fletcher concentrated on the lock-actuator mechanism —he insisted that the disk could be nothing but a lock —and described everything he thought and did for the benefit of Dodds, who was recording on the *Rhabwar*.

"The two rough areas inside the disk appear not to be corrosion," he said, "but in my opinion are patches of artificially roughened metal designed to give traction to the space-gauntleted mandibles or manipulatory appendages of the ship's crew—"

"I'm not so sure of that," said Conway. The idea he had had at the back of his mind was taking shape again.

"—to ease the operation of the actuator, this disk, that is," Fletcher continued, ignoring him. "Now, the disk may be turned clockwise or counterclockwise, screwed in or out on threads in either direction, pulled outwards, or pressed inwards and turned one way or the other into a locking position . . ."

The Captain performed the various twisting and pressing movements as he described them, but with no effect. He increased the power on his foot and wrist magnets so as to hold himself more firmly against the hull, placed his gauntleted thumb and forefinger on the two rough spots and twisted even harder. His hand slipped, so that momentarily all of the pressure was on his thumb and one rough area. That half of the disk tilted inwards while the other side moved out. The Captain's face became very red behind his visor.

" . . . or, of course, it might turn out to be a simple rocker switch," he added.

Suddenly the large, circular hatch began to swing inwards, and the ship's atmosphere rushed out through the opening seal. The fabric of the portable lock they had attached to the hull bellied outwards and the metal cylinder of its double seal drew away from them, allowing them to stand up inside a large, inflated hemisphere of transparent plastic. As they were watching the hatch move inwards and upwards to the ceiling of the ship's lock chamber, a short loading ramp was slowly extruded. It curved downwards to stop at the position that would have corresponded to ground level had the ship been on the ground.

Murchison had arrived and had been watching them through the portable lock fabric. "The air that escaped was from the lock chamber, because the flow has already stopped. If I could measure the volume of that lock chamber and our own portable job, I could calculate the aliens' atmospheric pressure requirements as well as analyze the constituent gases . . . I'm coming in."

"Obviously a boarding hatch," said the Captain. "They should have a smaller, less complicated lock for space EVAs and—"

"No," said Conway, quietly but very firmly. "These

people would not go in for extravehicular activity in space. They would be terrified of losing themselves."

Murchison looked at him without speaking, and the Captain said impatiently, "I don't understand you, Doctor. Prilicla, was there any emotional response from the survivors when we opened the lock?"

"No, friend Fletcher," the empath replied. "Friend Conway is emoting too strongly for the survivors to register with me."

The Captain stared at Conway for a moment, then he said awkwardly, "Doctor, my specialty has been the study of extraterrestrial mechanisms, control systems and communication devices, and my wide experience in this area led to my appointment to the ambulance ship project. The reason why I was able to operate this lock mechanism so quickly was partly because of my expertise and partly through sheer luck. So there is no reason why you, Doctor, whose expertise lies in a different area, should feel irritated just because—"

"My apologies for interrupting, friend Fletcher," said Prilicla timidly, "but he is not irritated. Friend Conway is feeling wonder, with great intensity."

Murchison and the Captain were both staring at him. Neither asked the obvious question, but he answered it anyway: "What would make a blind race reach for the stars?"

It took several minutes to make the Captain see that Conway's theory fitted all the facts as they knew them, but even then Fletcher was not completely convinced that the crew of the ship was blind. It was true that the rough areas on the vessel's underside, particularly those in the area of the thrusters, would give a being possessing only the sense of touch a strong tactual warning of danger, and that the smaller rough areas placed at regular intervals around the rim were probably the coverings of the less dangerous altitude jets. The smallest and most numerous patches of what at first they had thought was corrosion could well be opening or maintenance instructions on access panels, written in an extraterrestrial equivalent of Braille.

The total absence of transparent material, specifically direct vision ports, also gave support to Conway's theory, although it was not impossible that the ports were there but protected by movable metal panels. It was a very good theory, Fletcher admitted, but he preferred to believe that the ship's crew *saw* in a different part of the electromagnetic spectrum, rather than were completely blind.

"Why the Braille, then?" Conway asked. But Fletcher did not answer because it was becoming increasingly obvious on closer examination that the rough spots on the panels and actuators were not there simply to furnish traction—each one was an individual as a fingerprint.

Like the exterior of the ship, the lock interior was unpainted metal. The lock chamber itself was large enough for them to stand upright, but the two actuator disks visible below the inner and outer seals were only a few inches above deck level. There were also a number of short, bright scratches and a few shallow dents in evidence, as though something heavy with sharp edges had been loaded or unloaded fairly recently.

"Physiologically," said Murchison, "this life-form could be a weirdie. Is it a large being whose manipulatory appendages are at ground level? Or are they a small species whose ship was designed to be visited or used by a much more massive race? If the latter, then the rescue should not be complicated by xenophobic reactions on the part of the survivors, since they already know that there are other intelligent life-forms and that the possibility exists that an other-species group might rescue them."

"It is much more likely to be a cargo lock, ma'am," said the Captain apologetically, "and it is the cargo, rather than their extraterrestrial friends, if any, that was massive. Are we ready to go in?"

Without replying, Murchison switched her helmet spotlight to wide beam. The Captain and Conway did the same.

Fletcher had already checked that he could maintain two-way communication with Haslam and Chen outside the ship and with Dodds on the *Rhabwar* by touching the helmet antenna to the metal of the hull, in effect making the ship's structure an extension of his antenna. He knelt down and depressed the actuator, which was positioned just above deck level inside the outer seal. The hatch swung closed, and he repeated the operation on a similarly positioned actuator below the inner seal.

For a few seconds nothing happened. Then they heard the hiss of atmosphere entering the lock chamber, and they felt their suits becoming less inflated as air pressure built up around them. As the inner seal opened to reveal a stretch of dark, apparently empty corridor, Murchison was busy tapping buttons on her analyzer.

"What do they breathe?" Conway asked.

"Just a moment, I'm double-checking," Murchison replied. Suddenly she opened her visor and grinned. "Does that answer your question?"

When he opened his own helmet, Conway felt his ears pop at the slight difference in air pressure. "So, the survivors are warm-blooded oxygen-breathers with roughly Earth-normal atmospheric-pressure requirements. This simplifies the job of preparing ward accommodation."

Fletcher hesitated for a moment, then he, too, opened his visor. "Let's find them first."

They stepped into a metal-walled corridor, featureless except for a large number of dents and scratches on the ceiling and walls, which extended for about thirty meters toward the center of the ship. At the end of the corridor, lying on the deck, was an indistinct something that looked like a tangle of metal bars projecting from a darker mass. Murchison's foot magnets made loud scraping sounds as she hurried towards it.

"Careful, ma'am," said the Captain. "If the doctor's theory is correct, all controls, actuators, instruction or warning tags will have tactile indicators, and there is still power available within the ship; otherwise, the airlock mechanism would not have worked for us. If the crew live and work in complete darkness, you will have to think with your fingers and feet and not touch anything that looks like a patch of corrosion."

"I'll be careful, Captain," Murchison promised.

To Conway, Fletcher said: "The inner seal has an actuator just like the others under its lower rim." He directed his helmet light at the area in question, then indicated a smaller circle a few inches to the right of the actuator switch. "Before we go any farther I would like to know what this one does."

"Well," Conway said, "about the only thing we know for sure is that it isn't a light switch." He laughed as Fletcher depressed one side of the disk.

Murchison gave an unladylike grunt of surprise as bright yellow light flooded the corridor from an unseen source at the other end.

"No comment," said the Captain.

Conway felt his face burning with embarrassment as he muttered about the lights being for the convenience of non-blind visitors.

"If this was a visitor," said Murchison, who had reached the other end of the corridor, "then it was very severely inconvenienced. Look here."

The corridor made a right-angle turn at its inboard end, although access to the new section was blocked by a heavy barred grill, which had been twisted away from its anchor points on the deck and one wall. Behind the damaged grill, dozens of metal rods and bars projected at random angles into the corridor space from the walls and ceiling. But they did not pay much attention to the strange cage-like outgrowth of metal because they were staring at the three extraterrestrials who were lying in wide, dried-up patches of their body fluids.

There were two very different physiological types, Conway saw at once. The large one resembled a Tralthan, but less massive and with stubbier legs projecting from a hemispherical carapace, which flared out slightly around the lower edges. From openings higher on the carapace sprouted four long and not particularly thin tentacles, which terminated in flat, spear-like tips with serrated bony edges. Midway between two of the tentacle openings was a larger gap in the carapace, from which projected a head that was all mouth and teeth, with just a little space reserved for two eyes set at the bottom of deep, bony craters.

Conway's first impression was that the entity was little more than an organic killing machine.

He had to remind himself that the Sector General staff included several beings whose species were highly intelligent and sensitive while retaining the physical equipment that had enabled them to fight their way to the top of their home planet's evolutionary tree.

The other two beings belonged to a much smaller species with much less in the way of organic weaponry. They were roughly circular, just over a meter in diameter, and in cross section, a slim oval flattened slightly on the underside. In shape they very much resembled their ship, except that *it* did not have a long, thin horn or sting projecting aft or a thin, wide slit on the opposite side, which was obviously a mouth. The upper lip of the mouth was wider and thicker than the lower, and on one of the dead beings it was curled over the lower lip, apparently sealing the mouth shut. Both of the beings were covered on their upper and lower surfaces and around the rims by some kind of organic stubble, which varied in thickness from pin size to the width of a small finger. The stubble on the underside was much coarser than that on the upper surface, and it was plain that parts of it were designed for ambulation.

"It is clear what happened here," said the Captain. "Two members of the species that crew this ship died when the large one broke free because of inadequate restraints, and presumably the survivors Prilicla detected were unable to cope with the situation and released a distress beacon."

One of the smaller beings, which had sustained multiple incised and punctured wounds, lay like a piece of torn and rumpled carpet under its killer's hind feet. Its companion, although just as dead, had suffered fewer wounds and had almost made its escape through a low opening in the wall at deck level before being immobilized and crushed by one of its attacker's forefeet. It had also, before it died, been able to inflict several deep puncture wounds on the larger alien's underside, and its broken-off horn or sting was still deeply embedded in one of them.

"I agree," said Conway. "But one thing puzzles me. The blind ones appear to have modified their ship to accommodate the larger life-form. Why would they go to so much trouble to capture such a dangerous specimen? They must need it very badly or consider it extremely valuable for some reason to risk confining it with a blind crew."

"Possibly they have weapons that reduce the risk," Fletcher said, "longer range, more effective weapons than that horn or sting, which these two omitted to carry for some reason and died because of the omission."

"What kind of long-range weapon," asked Conway, "could be developed by a being with only a sense of touch?"

Murchison tried to head off the argument that was impending. "We don't know for certain that they have only a sense of touch, although they are blind. As for the value of the large life-form to them, it could be a fast-breeding source of food, or its tissues or organs might contain important sources of valuable medication, or the reason maybe a completely alien one. Excuse me."

She switched on her suit radio. "Naydrad, we have three cadavers to transfer to the lab. Move them in the litter to avoid additional damage to the specimens by decompression." She turned to Conway and the Captain. "I don't think the other members of the crew would object to my opening up their friends, especially since the large one has already begun the process."

Conway nodded. They both knew that the more she was able to discover about the physiology and metabolism of the two dead specimens, the better would be their chances of helping the surviving blind ones.

With Fletcher's help they extricated the large cadaver from its cage and from the strange assortment of metal rods and bars that were pressing it against the deck. They had to widen the opening it had made in the grill. This required the combined efforts of the three of them and gave some indication of the strength of the being who had forced it apart. When

they had the large alien free, its tentacles opened out
and practically blocked the corridor as it floated
weightless in the confined space.

While they were pushing it towards the airlock,
Murchison said, "The deployment of the legs and tentacles is similar to the Hudlar FROB life-form, but
that carapace is a thicker ELNT Melfan shell without
markings, and it is plainly not herbivorous. Considering the fact that it is warm-blooded and oxygen-
breathing and its appendages show no evidence of the
ability to manipulate tools or materials, I would tentatively classify it as FSOJ, and probably non-
intelligent."

"Certainly non-intelligent, considering the circumstances," said Fletcher as they returned to the caged
section of corridor. "It was an escaped specimen,
ma'am."

"We medical types," said Murchison, smiling, "never
commit ourselves, especially where a brand-new life-
form is concerned. But right now I wouldn't even try
to classify the blind ones."

Since she was the smallest person there, it was Murchison who wriggled carefully through the damaged
grill and between the projecting rods and bars. If it had
not been for the large alien warping a number of the
bars out of true, she would not have been able to
reach the blind one at all.

"This," she said breathlessly as she reached the
cadaver, "is a very strange cage."

Although it was brightly lit, they could not see the
other end of the caged section of corridor, because it
followed the curvature of the ship, which at this distance from the center was sharp enough to keep
them from seeing more than ten meters into it. The corridor walls and ceiling of the section they could see,
however, were covered with projecting metal bars and
rods. Some of them had sharp tips, others had spatu-
late ends and a few of them terminated in something
that resembled a small metal ball covered in blunt
spikes. The metal bars projected from slits in the walls,
and the slots were long enough to allow their individual
bars a wide angle of travel either up and down or from

side to side. The rods protruded from circular holes and collar pieces in the ceiling and were designed only to move in and out.

"It is strange to me, too, ma'am," said the Captain. "None of the e-t technology I've studied gives me any ideas. For one thing, it is a large cage, or should I say a very long cage, if it is continued around the ship. Perhaps it was meant to house more than one specimen, or the one specimen required space in which to exercise. I'm guessing, but I would say that the bars and rods projecting into the corridor formed some kind of restraint whereby the specimen could be immobilized in any part of the caged section for feeding purposes or for physical examination."

"A pretty good guess, I'd say," said Conway. "And if there was a malfunction in the mobile restraints, then the metal grill formed a safety backup that couldn't, on this occasion, withstand the specimen's attack. But I'm wondering just how far this corridor follows the radius of the ship. Extending this arc to the other side of the vessel places it in the area where Prilicla detected the two survivors. One of those survivors, according to Prilicla, was emoting anger on a very basic, perhaps animal, level while the other being's emotional radiation was more complex.

"Let's suppose," Conway went on, "that there is another large alien at the other end of the corridor cage, maybe even outside the other end of the cage, with a badly injured blind one who wasn't as successful as its crew-mate here in killing the brute—"

He broke off as Naydrad's voice sounded in the suit phones, saying that it was outside with the pressure litter.

Murchison pushed the first blind one towards the lock. "Wait for a few minutes, Naydrad, and you can load all three specimens."

Fletcher had been staring at Conway while the doctor was talking, plainly not liking the thought of another large FSOJ being in the ship. He pointed anxiously at the second blind one's body. "This one nearly escaped after killing the FSOJ with its horn. If we knew where

it was trying to escape to, we might know where to look
for its crew-mate who did escape."

"I'll help you," said Conway.

Time for the survivors, whichever species they belonged to, was fast running out.

At deck level there was a low rectangular opening,
which was wide and deep enough to allow entry to a
blind one. Nearly one third of its flat, circular body was
inside the opening, and when they tried to remove it
they encountered resistance and had to give the creature a gentle tug to pull it free. They were pushing it
towards Murchison, who was waiting to load it into the
airlock with the other two specimens, when there was
an interruption on the suit frequency.

"Sir! A panel is swinging open topside. It looks like
. . . it is an antenna being deployed."

"Prilicla," Conway called quickly, "the survivors.
Is one of them conscious?"

"No, friend Conway," the empath replied. "Both
remain deeply unconscious."

Fletcher stared at Conway for a moment. "If the
survivors did not extend that antenna, then we did,
probably when we were pulling the blind one out from
that opening." He bent suddenly and slid his foot magnets backwards until he was lying flat against the corridor floor. He moved his head close to the opening
through which the blind one had tried to escape, and
directed his helmet light inside. "Look at this, Doctor,
I think we've found the control center."

They were looking into a wide, low tunnel whose internal dimensions were slightly larger than those of
the bodies of the blind ones. Visibility was restricted
because, like the corridor behind them, it followed the
curvature of the ship. For a distance of about fifteen
inches inside the opening the floor was bare, but the
roof was covered with the tactually labeled actuators of
the type they had found in the airlock. There were,
naturally, no indicator lights or visual displays. Just
beyond this area the tunnel had no roof, and they had
a clear view of the first control position.

In shape it resembled a circular, elliptical sectioned
sandwich open around the edges to facilitate entry by

the blind ones of the crew. They could see hundreds of actuators covering the inside faces of the sandwich and, on the outer surfaces, the cable runs and linkages that connected the actuators with the mechanisms they controlled. The majority of the cable runs led towards the center of the ship while the rest curved towards the rim. There was no evidence of color-coding on the cables, but the sheathing carried various embossed and inset patterns that performed the same function for technicians who felt but could not see. A second control pod was visible beyond the first one.

"I can see only two control positions clearly," said Fletcher, "but we know that the crew numbered at least three. The survivor is probably out of sight around that curve, and if we could squeeze through the tunnel—"

"Physically impossible," said Conway.

"—without blundering against actuators every foot of the way," the Captain went on, "and switching on every system in the ship. I wonder why these people, who do not appear to be stupid, even if they are blind, placed a control position so close to the cage of a dangerous captive animal. That was taking a risk."

"If they couldn't keep an eye on it," said Conway dryly, "they had to keep closely in touch."

"Was that a joke?" the Captain asked disapprovingly while he detached one of his gauntlets and reached into the opening. A few seconds later he said, "I think I feel the actuator we must have snagged pulling the blind one out. I'm pressing it, now."

Chen's voice on the suit frequency broke in. "There is another antenna array deploying, close to the first one, sir."

"Sorry," said Fletcher. For a moment his face registered an expression of deep concentration as his fingers felt their way over the alien controls; then Chen reported that both antennae had retracted.

The Captain smiled. "Assuming that they group their controls together in sensible fashion, and the actuators for power, altitude control, life-support, communications and so on occupy their own specific areas on the control panels, I'd say that the blind one was touching its communications panel when it died. It managed to release a distress beacon, but that was probably the last thing it was able to do.

"Doctor," he added, "could you give me your hand, please?"

Conway gave his hand to the Captain to steady him and help him to his feet while Fletcher carefully withdrew his other hand from the opening. Suddenly one of Fletcher's foot magnets slipped along the deck. His arm jerked backwards instinctively to prevent him from falling, even though in the weightless condition he could not fall, sending the hand back inside the control area.

"I touched something." He sounded worried.

"You certainly did," said Conway, and pointed at the caged section of corridor.

"Sir!" said Haslam on the suit frequency. "We are detecting strong intermittent vibrations throughout the fabric of the ship. Also metallic sounds!"

Murchison came diving along the corridor from the airlock. She checked herself expertly against the wall. "What's *happening?*" Then she, too, looked into the caged corridor. "What *is* happening?"

For as far as they could see along the curvature of the corridor there was violent and noisy mechanical activity. The long metal bars projecting from their slots in the walls were whipping back and forth or up and down to the limits of their angles of travel, while the rods with their pointed or mace-like ends were jabbing up and down like pistons from the ceiling. Several of the bars and pistons were badly warped and were striking one another, which caused the awful din. As they watched, a small flap opened in the inboard wall of the corridor a few meters inside the grill, and a mass of something resembling thick porridge was extruded, to drift like a misshapen football into the path of the nearest wildly swinging bar.

The material splattered in all directions, and the smaller pieces were batted about by the other bars and pistons until they moved about the corridor like a sticky hailstorm. Murchison captured some of it in a specimen bag.

"Obviously a food dispenser of some kind," she observed. "An analysis of this stuff will tell us a lot about the large one's metabolism. But those bars and pistons are not, to my mind, a means of restraining the FSOJ. Not unless restraint includes clubbing it unconscious."

"With a physiological classification of FSOJ," said Conway thoughtfully, "that might be the only way to do it, short of using a heavy-duty pressor beam."

"All the same," Murchison went on, "I am feeling a slight attenuation of sympathy for the blind ones. That corridor looks more like a torture chamber than a cage."

Conway had been thinking the same thing and so, judging by his shocked and sickened expression, had the Captain. They had all been taught, and were themselves convinced, that there was no such thing as a completely evil and inimical intelligent race, and even the suggestion that they believed such a thing possible would have led to their dismissal from the Monitor Corps or from the Federation's largest multienvironment hospital. Extraterrestrials were different, sometimes wildly and weirdly different, and during the early stages of contact a great deal of caution was necessary until a full understanding of their physiological, psychological and cultural background was available. But there was no such thing as an evil race. Evil or antisocial individuals, perhaps, but not an evil species.

Any species that had evolved to the point of social and technological co-operation necessary for them to travel between the stars had to be civilized. This was the considered opinion of the Federation's most advanced minds, which were housed inside some sixty-odd different life-forms. Conway had never been the slightest bit xenophobic, but neither was he completely convinced that somewhere there wasn't an exception that would prove the rule.

"I'm going back with the specimens now," Murchison said. "I may be able to find some answers. The trouble is finding the right questions to ask."

Fletcher was stretched out on the deck again with one hand inside the control area. "I'll have to shut off that . . . whatever it is. But I don't know where exactly my hand was when I switched it on, or if I switched on anything else at the same time." He tripped his suit radio toggle. "Haslam, Chen. Will you chart the extent of the noise and vibrations, please, and is there evidence of any other unusual activity within the ship?" He turned to Conway. "Doctor, while I'm trying to find the right button to push, would you do something for me? Use my cutting torch on the corridor wall midway between the L-bend here and the airlock—"

He broke off as they were suddenly plunged into absolute darkness, which seemed to augment the clanging and metallic screeching sounds to such an extent that Conway fumbled for his helmet light switch in near panic. But before he could reach it the ship's lighting came on again.

"That wasn't it," said the Captain, then he continued: "The reason I want you to do this, Doctor, is to find an easier path to the survivors than the one along the corridor. You probably noticed that the majority of the cable runs originating in the control pods go inboard towards the power generation area of the ship, with very few leading out to the periphery. From this I assume that the area of the vessel outboard of the corridor cage and control center is the storage or cargo sections, which should, if the blind ones follow basic design philosophy where their spaceships are concerned, be comprised of large compartments connected by simple doors rather than pressurized bulkheads and airlocks. If this is so, and the sensor readings seem to confirm it, we should have to move only some cargo or stores out of the way to be able to bypass the control pods and get to the survivors fairly quickly. We would not have to risk running through that corridor, or worry about accidentally depressurizing the ship by cutting in from topside . . . "

Before the Captain had finished speaking, Conway began cutting a narrow vertical rectangle in the wall plating, a shape that would enable both his eyes and the helmet light to be directed through the opening at the same time so that he could see into the adjoining compartment. But when he burned through the wall there was nothing to see except a black, powdery substance,

which spilled out of the opening and hung in a weightless cloud until the movement of his cutter flame sent
it spinning into tiny three-dimensional whirlpools.

He worked his hand carefully into the hole, feeling
the warmth of the still-hot edges through his thin gauntlets, and withdrew a small handful of the stuff to ex-
amine it more closely. Then he moved to another
section of the wall and tried again. And again.

Fletcher watched him but did not speak. All of the
Captain's attention was again concentrated in his fingertips. Conway began working on the opposite wall of the
corridor, reducing the size of the test holes to speed up
the process. When he had cut four widely separated
fist-sized holes without uncovering anything but the
powdery material, he called Murchison.

"We are finding large quantities of a coarse black
powder," he told her, "which has a faint odor suggesting an organic or partly organic composition. It could
be a form of nutrient soil. Does that fit the crew's
physiology profile?"

"It fits," said Murchison promptly. "From my preliminary examination of the two small cadavers I would
say that the atmosphere in their ship is for the convenience of the larger FSOJ life-form. The blind ones do
not possess lungs as such. They are burrowers who
metabolize the organic constituents of their soil as well
as any other plant or animal tissue that happens to be
available. They ingest the soil via the large frontal
mouth opening, but the larger upper lip is capable of
being folded over the lower one so that the mouth is
sealed shut when it needs to burrow without eating.
We've noticed atrophy of the limbs, or to be more accurate, the movable pads on the underside that propel
it, and of hypersensitivity in the upper-surface tactual
sensors. This probably means that their culture has
evolved to the stage where they inhabit artificially
constructed tunnel systems with readily accessible food
supplies, rather than having to burrow for it. The material you describe could be a special loosely packed
nutrient soil that combines the ship's food supply with
a medium for physical exercise."

"I see," said Conway.

A blind, burrowing worm who somehow managed to reach the stars! Then Murchison's next words reminded him that the blind ones were capable of seemingly petty and cruel activities as well as those that were great and glorious.

"Regarding the survivors," she went on, "if the FSOJ laboratory animal, or whatever it is, is too close to the surviving crew-member and we cannot rescue both without endangering ourselves or the blind one, a large reduction in atmospheric pressure, provided it is carried out gradually so as to avoid decompression damage to the blind one's tissues, would disable or more likely kill the FSOJ."

"That would be the last thing we would try," said Conway firmly. The rules were very strict in first-contact situations like this, where one could never be absolutely sure that an apparently senseless and ferocious beast was, in fact, a non-sentient creature.

"I know, I know," Murchison replied. "And it will interest you to know that the FSOJ was in an advanced stage of pregnancy, a time during which most life-forms, regardless of their degree of intelligence, can feel overprotective, overemotional and overaggressive if they think their unborn is being threatened. That might be the reason why the FSOJ broke out of its cage. As well, the blind one would not have been able to kill it with its horn if the FSOJ's underbody had not been locally weakened in preparation for the imminent birth."

Conway considered that for a moment. "The female FSOJ's condition and the beating and prodding it had to take in the—"

"I didn't say it was female," Murchison broke in, "though it may be. In many ways it is a far more interesting life-form than the blind one."

"Save your mental energy for the one we *know* is intelligent," Conway snapped at her. There was a moment's silence, broken only by the background hiss from the suit radio. Then he said apologized: "Ignore me, please, I've got a bad headache."

"Me, too," Fletcher said. "I expect it is caused by the noise and subsonic effects of the vibration of all this

moving machinery. If his headache is half as bad as
mine you can forgive him, ma'am, and if you could
have some helpful medication ready when we return
to the ship—"

"Make that three," said Murchison. "My head has
been aching since I came back here, and I was exposed
to the noise and vibration for only a few minutes. And
I've bad news for you: The headache does not re-
spond to medication."

She broke contact. "Doesn't it seem strange,"
Fletcher asked worriedly, "that three people who
breathed the air in this ship are suffering from—"

"Back at the hospital," Conway broke in, "they have
a saying that psychosomatic aches are contagious
and incurable. Murchison's analyzer checked the ship's
atmosphere for toxic material, and any alien bugs
present are just not interested in us. This particular
headache could be a product of anxiety, tension, or a
combination of various psychological factors. But because it is affecting all three of us at once, and all three
of us have spent some time inside the ship, it is probable that the headache is being caused by some outside
agency, very likely the noise and vibration from that
corridor, and you were right the first time. I'm sorry I
mentioned it."

"If you hadn't," said Fletcher, "I certainly would
have done so. It is quite unpleasant and is affecting my
ability to concentrate on these—"

There was another interruption from the outer hull.

"Haslam, sir. Chen and I have finished charting the
extent of the sounds and vibration. They occupy a
narrow band, perhaps two meters wide, which coincides
with what you have called the corridor cage. The corridor runs right around the ship in a constant-radius
circle, which is completed by the arc containing the control pods. But that's not all, sir. The corridor intersects
the area occupied by the two survivors."

Fletcher looked at Conway. "If I could only stop
this mechanical torture chamber, or whatever it is,
we might be able to squeeze through it to the survivors
. . . But no, if it started up again when someone was

inside, it would batter them to death. Very well," he said to Haslam, "is there anything else to report?"

"Well, sir," Haslam replied hesitantly. "This may not mean anything, but we have headaches too."

For a long time there was silence while the Captain and Conway thought about the two *Rhabwar* officers' headaches. The men had been outside the ship at all times, making contact with the hull plating infrequently and then only through their magnetic boots and gauntlets—both of which had padded and insulated interiors capable of damping out mechanical vibration. Besides, sounds did not travel through a vacuum. Conway could think of nothing that would explain the two men's headaches, but not so the Captain.

"Dodds," Fletcher said suddenly to the officer he had left in the *Rhabwar*. "Run a sensor recheck for radiation emanating from this ship. It may not have been present until I started pushing buttons. Also, check for possibly harmful radiation associated with the nearby star cluster."

Conway gave a nod of approval, which the Captain did not see. Even flat on his back with a thumping headache making it difficult to think and with one arm disappearing into an alien control pod in which an unguarded touch could cause anything from the lights going out to an unscheduled Jump into hyperspace, Fletcher was doing all right. But the sensor reading, according to Dodds, cleared the alien ship and the space around them of any trace of harmful radiation. They were still thinking about this when the timid voice of Prilicla broke the silence.

"Friend Conway," called the empath, "I have delayed making this report until I was sure of my feelings, but there can no longer be any doubt. The condition of both survivors is improving steadily."

"Thank you, Prilicla," said Conway. "That will give us more time to think of a way of rescuing them." To Fletcher, he added, "But why the sudden improvement?"

The Captain looked at the corridor cage and its outgrowth of furiously waving and jabbing metal and said, "Could that have anything to do with it?"

"I don't know," said Conway, grinning in relief because the chances of a successful rescue had increased. "Certainly the noise alone is fit to wake the nearly dead."

The Captain looked disapprovingly at him, plainly unable to see anything funny in the remark or the situation. Very seriously, he said, "I have checked and rechecked all of the flat rocker switches within reach. That particular form of actuator is the only kind suited to the short feeler pads possessed by the blind ones, because as manipulators the pads lack strength and leverage. But I have found something that feels like a lever, several inches long and terminating in a narrow reverse-conical handle. The cone is hollow and is probably designed to accommodate the tip of the blind one's horn or sting. The lever is positioned at a forty-five-degree angle to its seating, which is the limit of its travel in the up direction. I intend moving it downwards.

"In case something calamitous happens as a result, we should seal our helmets," Fletcher added. He closed his helmet visor and replaced the gauntlet he had removed earlier. Then he reached inside the opening without hesitation, obviously knowing exactly where his hand was going.

In the corridor cage all mechanical activity ceased abruptly. The silence was so complete that when someone scraped a magnetic boot against the outer hull the noise made Conway start. The Captain was smiling as he got to his feet and opened his visor again.

"The survivors are at the other end of this corridor, Doctor," he said, then added, "if we can just get to them."

But they found it completely impossible to wriggle through the thicket of projecting metal rods and bars. Even when the Captain took off his spacesuit to try it, he was successful only in collecting a number of cuts and abrasions. Disappointed, Fletcher climbed into his suit again and began attacking the metal projections with his cutter. But the metal was tough and required several seconds at maximum power before each metal bar was burned through. There were so many of the things it was like weeding a metal garden a stalk at a time, the Captain observed crossly. He had cleared less than two meters of the corridor cage when they were forced back to the airlock because of the buildup of heat.

"It's no good," said the Captain. "We can cut a way through to them, but only in short stages with lengthy delays in between to allow the excess heat to dissipate by conduction through the fabric of the ship and to radiate into space. There is also the danger that the heat might melt the insulation on some of their power-control circuitry, with unknown results."

He tapped the wall beside him with his fist, so hard that it might almost have been a display of temper. "Emptying the storage spaces of nutrient soil would also be a long job, necessitating as it would the movement of the soil in installments from the storage spaces to the corridor to the lock and out, and we have no idea what structural problems could then arise inside those compartments. I'm beginning to think the only thing to do is cut a way in from outside. But there are problems there, too . . . "

Cutting down to the survivors through the double hull of the ship would generate a lot of heat, especially inside the portable lock they would have to use to guard against accidentally depressurizing the vessel. Once again, lengthy delays would be required to allow the heat to radiate away, although the process would be faster since they would already be on the outer hull. There was also the problem of cutting through the mechanical linkages to the bars and pistons projecting into the corridor, which would tend to generate a lot of heat inside the ship, heat which might have an adverse effect on the survivors. The only advantage was that they would not run the risk of being beaten to death by metal bars if as a result of their cutting operations the system switched itself on again.

" . . . And by the way, Doctor," Fletcher added, changing from his lecturing tone, "my headache is fading."

Conway was telling him that his own headache was diminishing as well when Prilicla broke into the conversation. "Friend Fletcher, I have been monitoring emotional radiation of the survivors since you halted the corridor mechanisms. Their condition has deteriorated steadily since then, and they are now in the state similar to that detected on our arrival, or perhaps a little worse. Friend Fletcher, we could easily lose them."

"That . . . that doesn't make sense!" the Captain burst out. He looked appealingly at Conway.

Conway could imagine Prilicla trembling inside its spacesuit at the Captain's outburst and the emotional radiation accompanying it. But he could just barely imagine the effort it had taken for the little empath, who found it acutely painful to disagree with anyone, to speak as it had. "Perhaps not," he said quickly to Fletcher, "but there is one way of finding out."

Fletcher gave him an angry, puzzled look, but he moved to the control pod opening and a few seconds later the noise and mechanical activity in the corridor had returned. So had Conway's headache.

Prilicla said, "The condition of the survivors is improving again."

"How much did they improve last time?" asked Conway. "And would you be able to tell by their emotional radiation if one being was about to attack another?"

"Both survivors were fully conscious for a few minutes," Prilicla replied. "Their radiation was so strong that I was able to reduce the area of uncertainty of their position. They are within two meters of each other, and neither of them was or is contemplating an attack."

"Are you telling me," the Captain said in a baffled tone, "that a fully conscious FSOJ and a blind one are as close together as that without the animal wanting to attack it?"

"Maybe the blind one found a locker or something to hide in," said Conway, "and to the FSOJ it is a case of out of sight, out of mind."

"Excuse me," said Prilicla. "There is no way that I can tell with absolute certainty that the two beings are of different species. The quality of their emotional radiation strongly suggests this. One is emoting anger and pain and little else while the other's emotions possess the complexity of a rational mind. But would it help you if you considered the possibility that they are both blind ones, one of whom has suffered gross brain damage, which is causing the raw, mindless level of emoting which I have detected."

"A nice theory, Doctor Prilicla," said the Captain. He winced and instinctively put his hands to his head, only to have them stopped short by his helmet. "It explains their close proximity, but it does not explain why their condition is affected by the corridor mechanisms. Unless I damaged the controls in some fashion, and accidentally made a connection between the corridor control lever and some emergency life-support equipment, perhaps a medical therapy unit or . . . I feel completely and utterly confused!"

"Everyone is feeling confused, friend Fletcher," said the empath. "The general emotional radiation leaves no doubt of that."

"Let's go back to the ship," said Conway suddenly. "I need some peace and quiet to think."

They left the blind ones' ship with Chen on watch with instructions to keep his distance and on no account to make physical contact with the vessel's structure. Prilicla returned with them, saying that the emotional radiation from the two survivors was strong enough for it to be monitored at a distance, since the condition of both was continuing to improve while the corridor mechanisms were still operating.

Entering by the Casualty Deck lock, they headed straight for the lab, which was occupied by a bloodstained Murchison and numerous pieces of FSOJ and blind ones spread around the dissecting tables. Naydrad joined them as Conway asked the Captain to project a plan view diagram of the blind ones' ship, incorporating the latest data. Fletcher looked relieved at having something to occupy him, since it was obvious that he did not share the close professional interest of the others in the pieces of extraterrestrial raw meat scattered about the place.

When the diagram appeared on the lab's display screen, Conway asked the Captain to correct him if he went wrong anywhere, then he began reviewing their problem.

Like most major problems this one was composed of a number of smaller ones, some of which were susceptible to solution. There was the blind ones' ship, which preliminary technical investigation showed to be structurally sound and in a fully powered-up condition. The vessel's configuration was that of a disk that tapered in thickness towards the circumference. At the center was a circle of perhaps one third the radius of the ship, which enclosed the power generation and associated equipment. Outside this area and enclosing it was a circular corridor linked to the airlock by a straight section of corridor, giving the appearance in the plan view of a sickle with a circular blade whose tip almost reached its handle. The short arc that joined the tip to the top of the handle was occupied by the control pods of the blind ones.

Beyond the circular corridor was the life-support area for both the crew and their captives. Proportionately, the volume of the ship devoted to the FSOJ life-form meant that the vessel had been designed specifically for the purpose of transporting these creatures. The lighting, atmosphere, FSOJ food dispenser and exercise space left no doubt about that.

Conway paused for a moment to look at Fletcher and the others, but there were no arguments. Then he went on: "The arrangement of rapidly moving bars and pistons in the caged corridor, particularly the ones with pointed and club-like extremities, worries me because I cannot accept the idea that the FSOJs are being used solely for the purpose of torture. I prefer the idea that they are being trained, perhaps domesticated, for a very special reason. One does not design an interstellar ship around a non-sentient life-form unless the creature is extremely valuable to the designers.

"We must therefore ask ourselves what the FSOJ has that the blind ones haven't," Conway went on. "What is it that they need most?"

They were all staring silently at the FSOJ cadaver. Murchison looked up at him suddenly, but it was the Captain who spoke first.

"Eyes?"

"Right," said Conway, then continued: "Naturally, I don't want to suggest that the FSOJs are the blind ones' equivalent of seeing-eye dogs. Rather, when their violent tendencies are curbed, a symbiotic or parasitic relationship is possible whereby the blind one attaches itself with its undersurface pads to tap into the FSOJ's central nervous system, in particular the vision network, so that it would receive—"

"Not possible," Murchison said firmly.

Prilicla began shaking to Conway's feelings of irritation and disappointment. His disappointment predominated because he knew that Murchison would not have spoken so bluntly had she not been certain of her facts.

"Perhaps with a surgical intervention as well as a training program . . ." Conway tried hopefully.

But Murchison shook her head. "I'm sorry," she said. "We now have enough information on both lifeforms to know that a symbiotic or parasitic relationship is impossible. The blind ones, which I have tentatively classified as CPSD, are omnivorous and have two sexes. One of the cadavers is male, the other female. The sting is their only natural weapon, but the poison sac associated with it has long since atrophied. I found scratches on the osseous tip of both stings, which suggests that they are now used as a manipulatory appendage. They are highly intelligent and, as we already know, technologically advanced despite their physical and sensory handicaps.

"Their only sense seems to be that of touch," she continued, "but judging by the degree of specialization apparent in the sensor pads covering the upper surface of their bodies, their touch is extremely sensitive. It is possible that some of those sensors would 'feel' vibrations in a solid or gaseous medium, or 'feel' the taste of substances with which they came in contact. As well as feeling, hearing and tasting after a fashion, a refinement of the 'taste' pads might also enable them to smell by touch. But they cannot see and would probably have difficulty in grasping the concept of sight, so they would not know a visual nerve network if they touched one."

Murchison indicated the opened torso of the FSOJ, then went on. "But that is not the principal reason why they cannot have a symbiotic relationship. Normally, an intelligent parasite or symbiont has to position itself close to the brain or in an area where the main nerve bundles are easily accessible. In our own case that would be at the back of the neck or the top of the head. But this beastie's brain is not in its skull; it is deep inside the torso with the rest of the other vital organs and is positioned in a rather stupid place, just under the womb and surrounding the beginning of the birth canal. As a result, the brain is compressed as the embryo grows, and if it is a difficult birth its parent's brain is destroyed. Junior comes out fighting and with a convenient food supply available until it can kill something for itself.

"The FSOJ, which is bisexual, retains its young in the womb until it is well-grown and fully equipped to survive," she added. "Survival cannot be easy where it lives, and the blind ones must have found a much more suitable life-form for a symbiont, if that was what they were looking for."

Conway rubbed his aching head and thought that difficult cases usually did not have this effect on him. Occasionally he had lost sleep over patients, or felt anxious or even seriously worried and tense when the time came to make a crucial decision in their case, but up until now it had never given him headaches. Was he growing old? But no, that was much too simple an explanation, because at the blind ones' ship they had all had headaches.

"One way or another we will have to go after the survivors," Conway said decisively. "And soon. But it would be criminal and stupid to endanger the life of a sentient being by wasting time on an experimental animal, even one that the ship's crew consider as valuable as the FSOJ. Now, if we agree that the FSOJ is non-sentient—"

"We depressurize the ship, wait until Prilicla says the FSOJ is dead and cut our way in to the surviving blind one as quickly as possible," the Captain finished for him, then added, "Dammit, my headache's back."

"A suggestion, friend Fletcher," said Prilicla diffidently. "The blind one is small and could probably negotiate the corridor cage without being inconvenienced by the FSOJ training mechanisms. The emotional radiation from both beings is increasing to the point where I would say that they are almost fully recovered. One is radiating anger of the insensate, uncontrolled kind while the other is feeling increasing frustration and is straining hard to do something. And I, too, am having some cranial discomfort, friend Conway."

The contagious headache again! thought Conway. *This is too much of a co-incidence . . .*

Suddenly his mind was back in time and space to his early years in the hospital, when he was insufferably proud to be on the staff of a multienvironment hospital even though at the time he was little more than a medical messenger boy. But then he had been given the assignment of liaison with one Doctor Arretapec, a VUXG who was teleportive, telekinetic and telepathic, and who had received Federation funding for his project of engendering intelligence in a race of nonsentient Saurians.

Arretapec had given Conway a headache in more ways than one.

He was only half-listening while the Captain was making the arrangements to depressurize the other ship. His plan was, first, to reposition the portable airlock above the survivors in case the blind one could not make its way along the corridor when the FSOJ was dead and they had begun the slow job of cutting a way in. But the sudden incredulity and anger in Fletcher's voice brought Conway's mind back to present time with a rush.

" . . . And *why* can't you do it?" the Captain was demanding. "Start moving that lock at once. Haslam and I will be over to help you in a few minutes. What's the matter with you, Chen?"

"I don't feel well," said Lieutenant Chen from his position beside the blind ones' ship. "Can I be relieved, sir?"

Before the Captain could reply, Conway said, "Ask

him if he has a headache of increasing severity, and is
there a feeling of intense itching originating deep inside
his ears. When he confirms this, tell him that the
discomfort will diminish with distance from the blind
ones' ship."

A few second later Chen was on his way back to
the *Rhabwar,* having confirmed Conway's description
of his symptoms. Fletcher asked helplessly, "What is
happening, Doctor?"

"I should have been expecting it," Conway replied,
"but it has been a long time since I had the experience.
And I should have remembered that beings who,
through physical damage or evolution, have been de-
prived of vital sensory equipment are compensated for
the loss. I think— no, I know. We are experiencing telepathy."

The Captain shook his head firmly. "You're wrong,
Doctor," he said. "There are a few telephathic races
in the Federation, but they tend to be philosophically
rather than technologically inclined, so we don't meet
them very often. But even I know that their ability to
communicate telepathically is confined to members
of their own species. Their organic transmitter and re-
ceivers are tuned to that one frequency, and other
species, even other telepathic species, cannot pick up
the signals."

"Correct," said Conway. "Generally speaking, telepaths communicate only with other telepaths. But
there have been a few rare exceptions recorded where
non-telepaths have received their thoughts for a few
seconds' or minutes' duration only, and more often than
not the experimenters suffered great discomfort without making contact at all. The reason for their partial
success is, according to the e-t neurologists, that many
species have a latent telepathic faculty that became
atrophied when they developed normal sensory equipment. But when my single, very brief experience
took place I had been working closely with a very
strong telepath on the same problem, seeing the same
images, discussing the same symptoms and sharing the
same feelings about our patient for days on end. We
must have established a temporary bridge, and for a

few minutes the telepath's thoughts and feelings were able to cross it."

Prilicla was shaking violently. "If the sentient survivor is trying to establish telepathic contact with us, friend Conway, it is trying very hard. It is feeling extreme desperation."

"I can understand that," said the Captain, "with a rapidly improving FSOJ nearby. Now what do we do, Doctor?"

Conway tried to make his aching head produce an answer before the surviving blind one suffered the same fate as its crew-mates. "If we could think hard about something we have in common with it. We could try thinking about the blind ones"—he waved his hand at the dissecting tables—"except that we might not have enough mental control to think of them whole and alive. If we thought about them as dissected specimens, however briefly, it would not be reassuring to the survivor. So look at and think about the FSOJ. As an experimental animal the blind one should not be bothered by seeing, feeling, experiencing or whatever, it in small pieces.

"I would like you all to concentrate on thinking about the FSOJ," he went on, looking at each of them in turn. "Concentrate hard, and at the same time try to project the feeling that you want to help. There may be some discomfort but no harmful after effects. Now think, think *hard* . . . !"

They stared at the partially dismembered FSOJ in silence, and thought. Prilicla began trembling violently and Naydrad's fur was doing strange things indeed as it reflected the Kelgian's feelings. Murchison's face turned white and her lips were pressed together, and the Captain was sweating.

"Some discomfort, he said," Fletcher muttered.

"Discomfort to a medic," said Murchison, briefly unclenching her teeth, "can mean anything from the pain of a sprained ankle to being boiled in oil, Captain."

"Stop talking," Conway snapped. "Concentrate."

His head felt as if it could no longer contain his aching brain and there was a raging itch growing inside his skull, a sensation he had felt just once before in his life. Conway glanced quickly at Fletcher as the Captain gave an agonized grunt and started poking at his ear with a finger. And suddenly there was contact. It was a weak, unspoken message that came from nowhere, but it was there in their minds as silent words that formed both a statement and a question.

"You are thinking of my Protector." . .

They all looked at each other, all obviously wondering if each had heard, felt, experienced the same words. The Captain let out his breath in an explosive sigh of relief, and said, "A . . . a Protector?"

"With those natural weapons," Murchison said, gesturing towards the FSOJ's horn-tipped tentacles and bony armor, "it certainly has the right equipment for the job."

"I don't understand why the blind ones need protectors," Naydrad said, "when they are technically advanced enough to build starships."

"They may have natural enemies on the home planet," began the Captain, "which they are incapable of controlling—"

"Later, later," Conway said sharply, breaking up what promised to become an interesting but time-wasting debate. "We can discuss this later when we have more data. Right now we must return to the ship. This must be extreme range for mind contact with nontelepaths like us, so we must get as close to it as possible. And this time we'll go for a rescue . . ."

With the exception of the Captain, the non-medical personnel remained with the ambulance ship. It was not thought that Haslam, Chen or Dodds could help very much unless or until they were required to burn a way into the other ship. Three extra minds that were not completely informed regarding the situation might, by their confused thinking, make it more difficult for the surviving telepath to communicate with the others, who, Conway thought dryly, were only slightly less confused than the crew-members.

Prilicla once again stationed itself near the hull to monitor emotional radiation in case the telepathy did not work. Fletcher carried a heavy-duty cutter intended, if necessary, to depressurize the ship rapidly and eliminate the Protector, and Naydrad had positioned itself with the pressure litter outside the airlock. In spite of their belief that the blind one could take decompression with much less danger than the FSOJ, Conway and Murchison would return with it inside the pressure litter should it require medical attention.

Their aching heads continued to feel as if someone were performing radical neurosurgery without benefit of an anesthetic. Since the few seconds of communication on the ambulance ship there had been nothing in their minds but their own thoughts and the maddening, itching headache, and there was no change as Murchison, Fletcher and Conway entered the lock chamber. As soon as they opened the inner seal, the noise of the corridor cage mechanisms thudding and screeching like an alien percussion section did nothing to improve their headaches.

"This time, try to think about the blind ones," said Conway as they moved inboard along the straight section of corridor. "Think about helping them. Try to ask who and what they are, because we need to know as much as possible about them if we are to help the survivor."

Even as he was speaking Conway felt that something was badly wrong, and he had an increasingly strong feeling that something terrible would happen if he did not stop and think carefully. But the raging, itching headache was making it difficult to think at all.

My Protector, the telepath on the ship had called the FSOJ. *You are thinking of my Protector.* He was missing something. But what?

"Friend Conway," Prilicla said suddenly. "Both survivors are moving along the corridor cage towards you. They are moving quickly."

They looked along the caged section with its screeching and clattering forest of waving metal bludgeons. The Captain unlimbered his cutter. "Prilicla, can you tell if the FSOJ is chasing the blind one?"

"I'm sorry, friend Fletcher," the empath replied. "They are close together. One being is radiating anger and pain, the other extreme anxiety, frustration and the emotional radiation associated with intense concentration."

"This is ridiculous!" Fletcher shouted above the suddenly increasing noise of the corridor mechanisms. "We have to kill the FSOJ if we're to rescue the blind one. I'm going to open the corridor to space—"

"No, wait!" said Conway urgently. "We haven't thought this through. We know nothing about the FSOJs, the Protectors. Think. Concentrate together. Ask, What are the Protectors? Who do they protect and why? What makes them so valuable to the blind ones? It answered once and it may answer again. Think hard!"

At that moment the FSOJ appeared round the curve of the corridor, moving rapidly in spite of the metal rods and clubs jabbing and battering at its body. The four horn-tipped tentacles whipped back and forth, pounding at the attacking metal bars and pistons and warping them out of shape, even tearing one of them out of its mounting. The noise was indescribable. The FSOJ was not quite running the course, Conway thought grimly as he saw the wounds overlaying the older scars on its body tegument and the distended underbelly, but it was moving fast, considering its condition. He felt a hand shaking his arm.

"Doctor, ma'am, are you both deaf?" Fletcher was shouting at them. "Get back to the airlock!"

"In a moment, Captain," said Murchison, shaking off Fletcher's hand and training her recorder on the advancing FSOJ. "I want to get this one tape. These aren't the surroundings I would choose in which to deliver my offspring, but then I suppose this one wasn't given any choice . . . Look out!"

The FSOJ had reached the section of corridor that had been partially cleared of the projecting metal by Fletcher's cutter. With nothing to stop it the being hurled itself through the damaged grill and was suddenly on them, floundering weightlessly now that the corridor mechanisms were no longer beating it against the floor, and spinning helplessly whenever a slashing tentacle struck the wall plating.

Conway flattened himself against the deck with his

wrist and boot magnets and began crawling backwards in the direction of the airlock. Murchison was already doing the same, but the Captain was still on his feet. He was retreating slowly and waving his cutter, which he had turned up to maximum intensity, in front of him like a fiery sword. One of the FSOJ's tentacles was badly charred, but the being did not appear to be handicapped in any way. Suddenly Fletcher gave a loud grunt as one of the FSOJ's tentacles hit him on the leg, knocking him away from magnetic contact with the deck and sending him cartwheeling helplessly.

Instinctively Conway gripped an arm as it came whirling past him, steadied the Captain, then pushed him towards the lock where Murchison was waiting to help him inside. A few minutes later they were all in the lock chamber and as safe as it was possible to be within a few meters of a rampaging FSOJ.

But it was a weakening FSOJ . . .

As they watched it through the partly open inner seal, the Captain checked the actuator of his cutter and aimed it towards the outer seal. His voice was slurred with pain. "That damned thing broke my leg, I think. But now we can hold the inner seal open, cut a hole through the outer one, and depressurize the ship fast. That'll fix the brute. But where's the other survivor? Where is the blind one?"

Slowly and deliberately, Conway covered the orifice of Fletcher's cutter with the palm of his hand. "There is no blind one. The ship's crew are dead."

Murchison and the Captain were staring at him as if he had suddenly become a mentally disturbed patient instead of the doctor. But there was no time for explanations. Slowly, and thinking hard about the words as he spoke them, he said, "We made contact with it once at long range. Now it is close to us and we must try again. There is so little time left to this being—"

The entity Conway is correct, came a soundless voice inside their heads. *I have very little time.*

"We mustn't waste it," said Conway urgently. He looked appealingly at Murchison and the Captain. "I think I know some of the answers, but we have to know more if we are to be able to help it. Think hard. What

are the blind ones? Who and what are the Protectors?
Why are they so valuable . . . ?"

Suddenly, they *knew*.

It was not the slow, steady trickle of data that
comes through the medium of the spoken word, but a
great, clear river of information that filled their minds
with everything that was known about the species from
its prehistory to the present time.

The Blind Ones . . .

They had begun as small, sightless, flat worms, burrowing in the primal ooze of their world, scavenging for
the most part, but often paralyzing larger life-forms
with their sting and ingesting them piecemeal. As they
grew in size and number their food requirements increased. They became blind hunters whose sense of
touch was specialized to the point where they did not
need any other sensory channel.

Specialized touch sensors enabled them to feel the
movements of their prey on the surface and to identify
its characteristic vibrations so that they could lie in
wait for it just below ground until it came within reach
of their sting. Other sensors were able to feel out and
identify tracks on the surface. This enabled them to
follow their prey over long distances to its lair and
either burrow underground and sting it from below, or
attack it while the sound vibrations it was making told
them it was asleep. They could not, of course, achieve
much against a sighted and conscious opponent on the
surface, and very often they became the prey rather
than the hunters, so their hunting strategy was concentrated on variations of the ambush tactic.

On the surface they "built" tracks and other markings of small animals, and these attracted larger beasts
of prey into their traps. But the surface animals were
steadily becoming larger and much too strong to be
seriously affected by a single Blind One's sting. They
were forced to co-operate in setting up these ambushes,
and co-operation in more ambitious food-gathering projects led in turn to contact on a widening scale, the
formation of subsurface food stores and communities,
towns, cities and interlinking systems of communication.
They already "talked" to one another and educated

their young by touch. Methods were even devised for augmenting and feeling vibrations over long distances.

The Blind Ones were capable of feeling vibrations in the ground and in the atmosphere, and eventually, with the use of amplifiers and transformers, they could "feel" light. They discovered fire and the wheel and the use of radio frequencies by transforming them into touch, and soon large areas of their planet were covered with radio beacons, which enabled them to undertake long journeys using mechanical transport. While they were aware of the advantages of powered flight, and a large number of Blind Ones had died experimenting with it, they preferred to stay in touch with the surface because they were, after all, completely unable to see.

This did not mean that they were unaware of their deficiency. Practically every non-sentient creature on their world had the strange ability to navigate accurately over short or long distances without the need of feeling the wind direction or the disturbances caused by vibrations bouncing off distant objects, but they had no real understanding of what the sense of sight could be. At the same time, the increasing sophistication of their long-range touching systems was making them aware that many and complex vibrations were reaching them from beyond their world, that there were sentient and probably more knowledgeable beings producing these faint touchings, and that these beings might be able to help them attain the sense that was possessed, seemingly, by all creatures except themselves.

Many, many more of the Blind Ones perished while feeling their way into space to their sister planets, but they learned eventually to travel between the stars they could not see. They sought with great difficulty and increasing hopelessness for intelligent life, feeling out world after world in vain, until finally they found the planet on which the Protectors of the Unborn lived.

The Protectors . . .

They had evolved on a world of shallow, steaming seas and swamps and jungles, where the line of demarcation between animal and vegetable life, so far as physical mobility and aggression were concerned, was unclear. To survive at all, a life-form had to move fast, and the dominant species on that world earned its place by fighting and moving and reproducing generations with a greater potential for survival than any of the others.

At a very early stage in their evolution the utter savagery of their environment had forced them into a physiological form that gave maximum protection to their vital organs—brain, heart, lungs, womb, all were deep inside the fantastically well muscled and armored body, and compressed into a relatively small volume. During gestation, the organic displacement was considerable because the embryo had to grow virtually to maturity before birth. It was rare that they were able to survive the reproduction of more than three of their kind; an aging parent was usually too weak to defend itself against attack by its last born.

But the principal reason why the Protectors rose to dominance on their world was because their young were well educated and already experienced in the techniques of survival before they were born. In the dawn of their evolution the process had begun simply as a transmission of a complex set of survival instincts at the genetic level, but the close juxtaposition of the brains of the parent and its developing embryo led to an effect analogous to induction of the electrochemical activity associated with thought. The embryos became short-range telepaths, receiving everything the parent saw or felt. And even before the growth of the embryo was complete, there was another embryo beginning to form within it that was also increasingly aware of the world outside its self-fertilizing grandparent. Then, gradually, the telepathic range increased, and communication became possible between embryos whose parents were close enough to see each other.

To minimize damage to the parent's internal organs, the growing embryo was paralyzed while in the womb, and the prebirth deparalyzing process also caused loss of sentience and the telepathic faculty. A newborn Protector would not last very long in its incredibly savage world if it was hampered by the ability to think.

With nothing to do but receive impressions from the

outside world, exchange thoughts and try to widen their telepathic range by making contact with various forms of non-sentient life around them, the embryos developed minds of great power and intelligence. But they could not build anything, or engage in any form of technical research, or do anything at all that would influence the activities of their parents and protectors, who had to fight and kill and eat unceasingly to maintain their unsleeping bodies and the unborn within them.

This was the situation when the first ship of the Blind Ones landed on the planet of the Protectors and made joyful mental and savage physical contact.

Immediately it became obvious that the two life-forms needed each other—the Blind Ones, technically advanced despite their sensory deprivation, and the highly intelligent race with two-way telepathy who were trapped inside the mindless organic killing machines that were their parents. A species who had just one sensory channel open, hyperdeveloped though it was, and with the capability of traveling between the stars; and another that was capable of experiencing all sensory impressions and of relaying those experiences, who had been confined to within a few square miles of its planetary surface.

Following the initial euphoria and heavy casualties among the Blind Ones, the short- and long-term plans were made for assimilating the Protectors into their culture. To begin with, the Blind Ones did not possess many starships, but a construction program for hyperships capable of transporting Protectors to the world of the Blind Ones was begun. There, although the environment was not as savage as that of their home planet, the surface was still untamed, because the Blind Ones perferred to live underground. There they would be positioned above the Blind Ones' subsurface cities, hunting and killing the native animals while their telepathic embryos absorbed the knowledge of the citizens below them, showing the Blind Ones what it was like to *see*, for the first time, the animals and vegetation, the sky with its sun, stars and constantly changing meteorological effects.

Much later, if the Protectors bred true on the Blind Ones' planet, small numbers would be used on the hyperships to help extend the range of their exploration and search for other sentient beings. But to begin with, the Protectors were needed as the eyes of the Blind Ones on their home world, and they were brought there by specially designed transports two at a time.

It was an extremely hazardous proceeding and many ships had been lost, almost certainly because of the escape of the Protectors from confinement and the subsequent death of the Blind Ones of the crew. But the greatest loss was that of the Protectors concerned and their precious telepathic Unborn.

On the present occasion one of the Protectors had broken out of the corridor cage and had been slow to lose consciousness when the beating and pummeling of its environmental support system had been withdrawn. It had killed one of the crew whose fellow crew-member had also been killed while going to its mate's assistance, then it had died accidentally on the second Blind One's sting. But before the Blind One died, it had released the distress beacon and deactivated the corridor cage mechanisms so as to render the surviving Protector unconscious, thus avoiding danger to any would-be rescuers until the telepathic embryo could explain matters.

But the Blind One had made two mistakes, neither of which were its fault. It had assumed that all races would be capable of making telepathic contact with the embryo as easily as had the Blind Ones, and it had also assumed that the embryo would remain conscious after its Protector became unconscious . . .

The great flood of data pouring into their minds had slowed gradually. It became specific rather than general, a clear, narrow conversational stream.

. . . *The Protector life-form is under constant attack from the moment of its birth until it dies,* the silent voice in their minds went on, *and the continuous physical assault plays an important part in maintaining the physiological system at optimum. To withdraw this violent stimulation causes an effect analogous to*

strangulation, if I read the entity Conway's mind cor-
rectly, including greatly reduced blood pressure, dimin-
ished sensoria and loss of voluntary muscle activity.
The entity Murchison is also thinking, correctly, that
the embryo concerned is similarly affected.

When the entity Fletcher accidentally reactivated
the corridor mechanisms, the return to consciousness
of my Protector and myself was begun, then checked
again when they were switched off, only to be turned
on again at the insistence of the entity whom you call
Prilicla, whose mind I cannot contact although it is
more sensitive to my feelings than my thoughts. Those
feelings were of urgency and frustration because I had
to explain the situation to you before I died.

While there is still time I would like to thank you
with all the remaining strength of my mind for making
contact, and for showing me in your minds the mar-
vels which exist not only on my planet and the world
of the Blind Ones, but throughout your Federation.
And I apologize for the pain caused while establishing
this contact, and for the injury to the entity Fletcher's
limb. As you now know, I have no control over the
actions of my Protector . . .

"Wait," said Conway suddenly. "There is no reason
why you should die. The life-support systems, your
corridor mechanisms and food dispensers are still operative and will remain so until we can move your ship
to Sector General. We can take care of you. Our resources are much greater than those of the Blind
Ones . . . "

Conway fell silent, feeling helpless despite his confident offer of help. The Protector's tentacles were
lashing out weakly and in haphazard fashion as it
drifted weightless and obviously dying in the center of
the corridor, and each time one of them struck the wall
or deck the reaction sent it spinning slowly. There was,
therefore, a good if intermittent view of the whole
birth process as first the head and then the four tentacles appeared. As yet, the Unborn's limbs were limp
and unmoving because the secretions that would release the prebirth paralysis, and at the same time
obliterate all cerebral activity not associated with sur-

vival, had not taken effect. Then, abruptly, the tentacles twitched, threshed about and began pulling the recently Unborn out of its parent's birth canal.

The soundless voice in their minds returned, but this time it was no longer sharp and clear. There was a feeling of pain and confusion and deep anxiety muddying up the clear stream of communication, but fortunately the message was simple:

To be born is to die, friends. My mind and my telepathic faculty are being destroyed, and I am becoming a Protector with my own Unborn to protect while it grows and thinks and makes contact with you. Please cherish it . . .

There had been some crepitation associated with the Captain's fractured tibia, and Conway had administered a strong painkiller to make him comfortable during the trip back to the ambulance ship. Fletcher remained fully conscious, and because of the relaxing of inhibitions that was a side effect of the medication, he talked continuously and anxiously about the Unborn telepaths and the Blind Ones.

"Don't worry about them, Captain," Murchison told him. They had moved Fletcher to the Casualty Deck, and she was helping Naydrad remove his spacesuit while Conway and Prilicla assembled the tools necessary for a piece of minor structural repair work. She went on: "The hospital will treat them with tender, loving care, never fear, although I can just imagine O'Mara's face when he learns that they have to be accommodated in what amounts to a torture chamber. And no doubt your Cultural Contact people will be there, too, hoping to obtain the services of a wide-range telepath . . ."

"But the Blind Ones need them most of all," Fletcher went on worriedly. "Just think of it. After millions of years in darkness they've found a way of seeing, even if their eyes can turn and quite literally kill them."

"Given a little time," Murchison said reassuringly, "the hospital will turn up the answer to that, too. Thornnastor just loves puzzles like this one. The continuous conception business, for instance, the embryo within an embryo. If we were able to isolate and inhibit the effects of the secretion that destroys the sentient portion of the Unborn's brain prior to birth, we would have telepathic Protectors as well as Unborn. And if the environmental beating they take all their lives was toned down gradually and eventually eliminated, they might get out of the habit of trying to kill and eat everything they see. The Blind Ones would have the telepathic eyes they need without danger to themselves, and they could roam all over the Galaxy if they wanted to."

She paused to help Naydrad cut away the trouser leg of the Captain's uniform, then addressed Conway. "He's ready for you now, Doctor."

Murchison and Naydrad were in position, and Prilicla was hovering above them, radiating feelings of reassurance. Conway said, "Relax, Captain. Forget about the Blind Ones and the Protectors. They will be all right. And so will you. After all, I'm a senior physician in the Federation's most advanced multienvironment hospital. But if you really feel the need to worry about something, think about my present problem." He smiled suddenly, and added, "It must be ten years since I last set a fractured DBDG tibia."

About the Author

JAMES WHITE was born in Belfast, Northern Ireland, and resides there, though he spent his early years in Canada. His first story was printed in 1953. He has since published well-received short stories, novellas and novels, but he is best known for the Sector General series, which deals with the difficulties involved in running a hospital that caters to many radically different life-forms.

Exciting Space Adventure from DEL REY